CAROUSEL
Chris Turnbull

ISBN-13: 978-1535313216

ISBN-10: 1535313218

First published 2016 by Chris Turnbull, YORK (UK)
Text © 2016 Chris Turnbull
Cover Design © 2016 Wicked Book Covers

For the real Camille,

I hope you grow up just as loving and strong minded as the book character.

To Anne & Olivier – I couldn't resist

I would also like to dedicate this book to those who lost their lives in the November 2015 Paris Attacks. – prise trop tôt

ALSO BY CHRIS TURNBULL

The Vintage Coat

D: Darkest Beginnings
D: Whitby's Darkest Secret
D: Revenge Hits London

It's Beginning To Look A Lot Like Christmas

A Home For Emy – Children's Book

CAROUSEL

Happy Reading !

[signature] Turnbull
x
2024.

Chapter ONE

Jonathan looked at his watch as he hurried back into the bedroom – 14.36pm, he was running late. Today was his wedding day, and he was already in his suit waiting for his best man Paul who was supposed to have picked him up over half an hour ago. The ceremony began at 3 o'clock and he couldn't be late. As he began searching Paul's number on his phone, a loud car horn blasted from outside his window. It was Paul, at last.

'Where have you been?' Jonathan barked upon entering the car, his voice on edge. His palms were clammy and his throat dry.

'Sorry mate, the car broke down and I had to borrow my brother's instead. Don't worry though, the church is only a ten-minute drive, we'll make it.' Paul had always been the calm one of Jonathan's friends, nothing ever seemed to faze him; hence him landing the job of best man. They drove out of the driveway in an old cream 1960s Volkswagen Beetle. All it needed was the number fifty-three on the front and it would have looked identical to the famous Herbie car. Still, it was much better than being late.

It was a Sunday, so the traffic was fairly quiet, and they pulled up outside the small village church with time to spare. It was early March and the lawn circling the small church was filled with hundreds of daffodils. The trees surrounding the stone building were lush with pink and white blossom that occasionally dropped in the breeze, falling like snowdrops onto the road. Jonathan leaped out of the car and sprinted up the uneven pathway, crashing into the enormous bright red doors before entering the church. The sound of the organ instantly filled his ears as it echoed through the central nave, and the wooden floor vibrated under his feet. As he walked down the aisle, the murmur of people talking turned to a hushed silence, and all eyes fell upon him.

The seating throughout the small church was already completely full, and Jonathan spotted his parents sitting up front, his mother smiling. Across the aisle were Nicola's parents, looking rather less excited; they had kicked up a fuss about how far they'd had to drive for the occasion, and they believed their daughter should have been married in the church close to where she had grown up in Yorkshire; which was conveniently close by to their own house. Nicola had a large family, and they took up a large portion of the guest list. Jonathan's smaller clan barely took up three rows.

Paul came pounding through the doorway behind. He slapped Jonathan on the back and said, 'I told you we would make it.' His boyish outlook was a trait he was renowned for.

They stood at the top of the aisle together, gesturing hellos to people as they waited. Seeing his family all dressed in their best, their faces smiling up at him in his suit, Jonathan felt a lump in his throat. He had been dating Nicola for nearly six years, and although he never thought he would be, he was emotional.

3 o'clock soon arrived and Nicola was yet to arrive. 'Typical', said Jonathan, looking at his watch. He knew how much she liked to make an entrance.

It was nearly quarter past when one of the bridesmaids finally peeked her head around the doorway. Jonathan did not see her, but Paul caught her eye immediately. She gestured for him to come to her, and without saying a word to Jonathan, he quickly made his way back up the aisle, leaving Jonathan wondering what was going on. The few minutes Paul was out of the room felt like an eternity to Jonathan. What on earth was happening?

When Paul re-entered, he gestured Jonathan over. His stomach was already doing summersaults; his mouth dry and his hands were shaking.

'What's going on?' Jonathan asked in a hushed tone, trying to ensure his voice didn't echo back to where his family were sat. Regardless, they all turned in their seats, looking at Jonathan with questioning expressions upon their faces.

'She's not coming mate.' Paul's words stabbed at Jonathan. 'That was her sister Amy; apparently she is refusing to leave the hotel.' Jonathan rushed at the door, hoping that Amy was still outside, but upon exiting the church he saw Amy pulling away in her little red Citroen. Standing in the churchyard, Jonathan dropped to his knees, throwing his face into his hands. Paul ran to him and placed a hand on his friend's shoulder. 'I am so sorry mate.' His usually boyish sarcasm could not have been more absent. Paul helped Jonathan to his feet, embracing him as he began to gently sob.

'Here.' Paul reached into his jacket pocket. 'Take the car keys and get yourself out of here. I will explain everything to the guests – you go home and I will call around later.'

Jonathan snatched the keys from his friend's grip without hesitation and headed for the little car. Loosening his purple tie, he allowed it to drop to the floor, and before entering the car he pulled off the oversized flower that had been secured to his jacket and threw it into the passenger footwell.

Paul stood and watched as Jonathan pulled out of the churchyard and took off down the street at full acceleration. He sighed and turned back to the church. His mind racing as he tried to come up with what to say to the waiting guests.

Jonathan drove straight past the end of his street. He did not want to go home, did not want to be alone; he contemplated driving to Nicola's hotel in a bid to speak to his fiancée, but quickly decided against it. He was not in the best of moods to speak to her rationally, and he certainly didn't want to make things worse.

Jonathan kept driving with no real destination in mind. His own thoughts raced around in his head at what had just happened. He was nearly thirty years old, and this was supposed to be the start of happiest year of his life. After being unemployed for nearly three years due to the collapse of the global economy, he was back in work again as a mechanic. He had started working with a company who restored old vintage cars. Cars from all walks of life were sent from across the United Kingdom to not only be fixed, but to be restored to their former glory. He had started back in October and after nearly six months was finally starting to see his life getting back on track. He and Nicola had even had a discussion before Christmas about starting a family, and she had come off of the pill in time for their honeymoon, which was supposed to see them fly to the Seychelles tomorrow.

Jonathan found himself driving in circles. Why was this island so small? He swore, and slammed his hands hard against the steering wheel. The isle of Jersey where he lived was only five miles long and nine miles wide, so a road trip any further would involve a ferry ride out or a flight from the small airport. Jonathan loved his life here; he had lived here his entire life, but he was slowly starting to crave more freedom than the small island could provide. Something felt missing to him – it had been playing on his mind for some time, but he could not figure out quite what it was he craved.

It was nearly an hour later when he finally stopped the car. He hadn't taken much notice as to where he was going, and found himself up against the coast, on the clifftops overlooking the calm blue water. The rattle of the rusty Beetle died as he turned off the engine, and Jonathan sat there for a moment, his thoughts momentarily absent as he stared out to sea. For a second then he felt calm until reality kicked back in. The wind was starting to pick up and the jagged rocks below bore the scars of the crashing tide that battered against it.

Jonathan exited the car and strode over towards the cliff edge. Peering over, he was startled by the scale of the drop, and immediately jumped backwards. He wasn't sure exactly where he was – he had never been to this area before, and he couldn't see any houses nearby. The road was a mere dirt track that led seemingly to nowhere.

The fresh salty air felt good against his face, and the late afternoon sun felt unusually warm for the time of year. Jonathan began to walk along the cliff top. There was no sign of a nearby town, yet the sea air and quiet clifftops lured him on.

As he walked his mind began racing; questions as to why Nicola did not want to marry him centred his thoughts. Was it something he had done? Or worse, was it something she had done? It wouldn't be the first time she had cheated on him, but he had forgiven her mistake all those years ago. Nonetheless, it still lingered on his mind.

The breeze blew through Jonathan's hair, and his white shirt danced in the wind; with his eyes closed tight he breathed and exhaled hard, the sea salt lingering in his nostrils. He peered into the fading sun and, despite everything, smiled to himself. Before he knew it, the early spring sun was already beginning to set; and he looked quickly at his watch in surprise. 'Surely it's not sunset already.' He spoke aloud to himself. The sea air was also beginning to cool, and Jonathan was starting to regret leaving his jacket in the car. He had been walking for nearly two hours when he finally came to a stop. In the dimming light he spotted a small village up ahead, and as he tried to figure out where he might be, the cloud-filled sky above opened up along the coast with an almighty downpour. A curtain of heavy rain could be seen approaching Jonathan, a monsoon like downpour that was approaching from the sea at an alarming speed.

Jonathan took off at speed in the direction of the village in hope of reaching shelter. As the small village grew closer, Jonathan could see it was a sleepy fishing port, with small houses that lined a narrow river leading out to sea. The rain began to fall hard as Jonathan finally left behind the slippery grass banks and reached a gravelled road, he was unexpectedly faced with a small amusement park shrouded in darkness. The rain came heavier still and began to blind Jonathans' vision. It was becoming unsafe to be out in this horrendous downpour as the road was quickly transformed into a raging river that was already reaching above Jonathan's ankles. He hurried through the amusement park gates, squinting through the rain in the hope to find somewhere to take shelter. As he ran through the numerous puddles of the gravelled surface, his smart wedding shoes slipped upon the water-sodden ground and he landed in a heap on the floor. Hurting only his pride, Jonathan got back to his feet, and before him he saw an impressive-looking carousel. He darted for it and leaped upon its wooden frame, heading past the outer horses to hide beneath its roof. He held onto one of the horses tight as he regained his breath.

His hair, once quaffed, was now soaked and flattened, while his white shirt was dirtied up the back from his fall and slightly transparent on the front through sheer wetness, his athletic torso so clear that he may as well have been shirtless. Jonathan wiped the water running down his face and watched as the downpour continued; it did not look as though it would be stopping anytime soon.

It had been nearly four hours since he had received the news about his bride-to-be not arriving at the church, and it was only now that Jonathan had finally stopped that the reality of what had happened began to sink in. He had no more questions running through his mind, no more anger burning inside him; only sorrow.

He burst into tears, something even he was surprised at. His entire body shook as the cold damp clothing started to turn his body numb. His sobs echoed off of the dome of the carousel. Jonathan sniffed deeply and quietened – he'd thought for a second that he had felt the carousel move. He stood there in silence for a moment, the sound of the rain bouncing against the carousel's top; it was the only sound he could hear over his own heavy breathing. Jonathan laughed to himself. He was losing it.

He took a deep breath and exhaled, but

before he could do anything more the carousel all of a sudden lit up. Jonathan started, his eyes closing against the sudden blinding light. As he tried to focus his eyes, the carousel made a loud creaking noise and began to move. Jonathan made for the edge but the carousel gained speed at an alarming rate, spinning around faster and faster still. Jonathan grabbed hold of one of the mechanical horses by the gold handrail. 'What the hell?' He cursed out loud. Faster and faster the carousel continued to spin. Fear began to spread through his chest as nausea began to swell in his stomach. There was a large clang, as through a spring had broken. The carousel slowly began to decrease in speed. Jonathan waited until the ride had come to a slow enough speed for him to jump off, and upon landing on the hard ground he immediately vomited.

He lay on his back, trying to steady his wobbly legs and his racing heart. As he lay there, he realised that not only had the rain stopped, but that the ground beneath him was no longer wet. He sat up quickly and realised that the gravel was also missing and had been replaced by dry, hard, dusty soil. He looked up at the carousel that was still in full glow.

The name 'Le Cheval Carrousel Volant' was painted along the top. It didn't take Jonathan long to realise that he was no longer in the amusement park. He appeared to be in what looked like an attractively well-kept park garden with rows and rows of lush trees surrounding him in perfect lines. But how had he gotten here? And where was he?

Chapter TWO

Jonathan stood, wiping down the sand-like soil from his clothing, and realised that he was completely dry. His white shirt and smart black trousers that had been sodden were as clean and dry as when he'd first put them on, despite the dusty soil he brushed from his trousers. A gentle breeze caused the leaves to rustle, and the sunlight squeezed through the branches like tiny spotlights reaching down to the ground.

Jonathan could see a larger lawned area beyond the last row of trees and began making his way towards it in the hope to see something familiar. He was still slightly dazed, and walked slowly to the edge of the tree line. Upon stepping into the sunlight he was instantly blinded by the sudden brightness. The blue sky above was clear from clouds, and the heat from the sun felt warmer than it had in a long time. He raised his hand to shade his eyes and gasped at what he saw before him. Across a wide cobblestone road, beyond a walled-off and low-lying river, Jonathan's eyes met the world's most recognisable landmark, the Eiffel tower.

'How in the hell am I in Paris?' Jonathan said out loud. His mouth was wide open as he took in the vast monument before him, his mind blank as he tried to come to terms with where he was. After a moment's silence, Jonathan began to walk in the direction of the tower, and as though somebody had just called 'Action' upon a film set, the road in front of him burst into life. Horse-drawn carriages raced along the cobbles, the horses' hooves clattering against the hard surface and the drivers shouting instructions to go faster, each one trying to overtake the next; clearly there was no right and wrong side of the road as carriages hurtled past each other from any direction. Jonathan stepped out onto the busy road, but instantly jumped back as a tram came whizzing towards him, rusty wheels rattling along the thin tracks and loud passengers chatting on the open-topped upper deck.

As Jonathan took in the sights before him, he couldn't help but notice that most people seemed to be wearing very similar clothing. The men all wore black suits with bowler hats or top hats, with a white shirt and tie. The women wore mostly dark-coloured floor length dresses or skirts that came in at the waist, and their tops featured long sleeves and high neck lines. This ensemble was topped off with a variety of hats of all different shapes and sizes; some woman where even carrying large umbrellas to shade themselves from the sun. Jonathan smirked to himself; he couldn't help but think it looked like a scene from a Charles Dickens story. It certainly looked as though he had stepped onto a film set – there was not a single modern car or piece of clothing to be seen anywhere. What on earth was going on?

Eventually, after a few hesitant attempts, he managed to cross the road where he perched himself against the wall that ran along the roadside and created a barrier between the road and the river below. His breath caught in his throat as one of the horse-drawn carriages mounted the narrow pavement to avoid an oncoming tram and nearly knocked him flying. Jonathan took off again in the direction of the bridge and away from the main road; the bridge lead straight across the river and towards the foot of the tower. Half way across the bridge he stopped; he could sense the people passing by were staring at him, and it took Jonathan a few moments to realise what it was. All the other men were wearing a jacket and hat, but he simply had on his white shirt and trousers. Jonathan placed both his hands on the railing and took in the sight of the water running slowly beneath him. A cool breeze brushed against his face.

'This has to be a dream,' he whispered to himself. Raising his hand to his face, he rubbed his eyes hard. When he opened his eyes the sight of the large metal-framed tower still dominated his view.

'I must have knocked myself out when I fell next to the carousel, I need to wake up.'
Jonathan slapped himself hard across the face. Despite the pain and the visible red mark now starting to appear across his face, he was still in Paris. 'I know

what always wakes me from a dream,' Jonathan again spoke aloud to himself, 'Falling!'

He again looked over the side of the bridge. The drop was certainly high enough to knock the wind out of anybody who jumped. Jonathan swallowed hard.

He took hold of the wide bridge railings and began climbing them. Using a large street lamp that formed part of the railing, he steadied himself carefully. Once on top, Jonathan took one final glance at the tower, before leaning his body towards the deep water below. He closed his eyes and allowed gravity to do the rest.

He had barely had his eyes closed for a second when, instead of falling forwards, he was falling backwards. The commotion of the horses and pedestrians still rang out in his ears, but as he landed hard against the pavement a new voice was heard above all the rest.

'À quoi tu joues?' the voice shouted into Jonathans ear. He knew French fluently as his grandmother was originally from Normandy, but he had not used it since before she passed away. Jonathan sat up from the ground and turned to look at the man who'd spoken to him.

'Err… I beg your pardon Sir?' Jonathan spoke in his best French dialect. He squinted as the sun shone in his eyes from behind the man's head.

'I said, what are you playing at? You could have gotten yourself killed.' The man spoke with a concerned tone. He moved around Jonathan and helped him to his feet. He, like many of the other men around, wore a black suit and tie with a bowler hat. He was young, younger than Jonathan with a lean physique. His short black hair was slicked back. But the thing that made this gentleman stand out from all the others was his impressive handlebar moustache that sat flawlessly above his top lip. It curled upwards at the end, and matched his thick bushy eyebrows that lined up perfectly above his dark brown eyes. He smiled at Jonathan warily and held out a hand to be shaken.

'My name is Samuel Baudin.' He reached out and grasped Jonathans hand.

'I am Jonathan, Jonathan Snow. Pleased to meet you.'

'You are British, Mister Snow?' Jonathan smirked at this – clearly his French was not as good as he'd thought.

'I am Sir, yes. But please, call me Jonathan.'

'Well Jonathan, can I help you in any way? After all, you did nearly just throw yourself off a bridge.' Samuel looked at Jonathan with concern in his face; he clearly had no intention of leaving him alone. His handlebar moustache made him look older than he probably was, yet his eyes had a young sparkle to them and his smile was boyish. Jonathan placed him in his mid-twenties, only a couple of years below himself.

'Where are you staying?' Samuel asked, tapping his foot idly.

'I've only just arrived in Paris, so I haven't really thought about that yet.' Samuel shook his head and sighed.

'I know a little place where you can stay for the night, come with us.' And he took hold of Jonathan's arm and turned him on the spot, where he was instantly faced with a young woman in a long navy blue dress. Beside her was a young boy of about four years old. 'This is my wife Sophia,' Samuel pointed, 'and this is our son, Frédéric.'

'A pleasure to meet you both,' said Jonathan with a slight nod of the head; Sophia gave a shy smile and looked down at her son who clung tightly to her dress. He had the lightest blonde hair, which matched that of his mother, and his large blue eyes looked at Jonathan curiously.

Samuel led his family and Jonathan across the road towards a small crowd of people, and within seconds a large black tram stopped in front of them. Samuel pushed his family aboard ahead of him, and gestured for Jonathan to follow. The tram was already busy, and inside Jonathan found himself pushed up against a dirty window. He could barely make out the passing scenery as the tram took off again along the road. Very few people spoke on the tram; it was packed so tightly that Jonathan wondered if anybody could actually breathe, let alone see when to get off.

The further the tram went, the more people began to dismount. It was twenty minutes before Samuel final reached past Jonathan to pull the wire cord that rang the bell. Again he ushered his family to the door ahead of him, but kept looking back to make sure Jonathan wasn't far behind.

As the tram sped away, Jonathan found himself on a quiet narrow street, the cobbled road only wide enough to fit one tram at a time. Samuel and his wife Sophia did not speak as they began walking the slim footpath with their young son between them. Jonathan hesitated for a moment – what was he doing following these people he did not know? How had he even arrived in Paris? One thing he had decided was that he probably was not dreaming.

The visible sky between the adjacent buildings was turning a warming shade of red as dusk began to set in. When Jonathan finally looked back at the street he was shocked to see Samuel and his family already so far ahead. He took off after them, afraid he would end up lost in the darkening streets. The family turned a corner onto yet another narrow street, and after a few more minutes the narrow street opened up into a beautiful square full of trees and luscious grass at its centre. It was not very large, but was sat perfectly hidden between the rows of four-storey buildings on one side and six-storeys on the other, casting the beautiful green into shadow.

Samuel took out a bulky set of keys and began unlocking a large wooden double-fronted door that sat at the bottom of one of the large six-storey buildings. Jonathan stood gazing up at it. There were enormous windows that each had a small railing attached, and a variety of potted plants that decorated the front of the building with shades of green interspersed with sudden bursts of pink or yellow.

Samuel gave an impatient cough as he stood in the doorway for Jonathan, who quickly snapped out of his own thoughts and dashed through the open doorway. Inside, he stood by a large marble stairwell that looked as though it would go straight up to the roof. Nestled between the stairs was a metal cage that took Jonathan a few moments to realise was an elevator shaft. Sophia and Frédéric could already be heard climbing the staircase, whilst Samuel ensured the front door was properly bolted up. He gave Jonathan a friendly slap on the shoulder as he passed and gestured for him to follow.

Once they had reached the second floor, Samuel stopped. Jonathan saw that there were two doors on this floor adjacent to one and other; one was wide open and the voice of young Frédéric could be heard inside.

'This is where my family and I live.' Samuel gestured towards the doorway. 'I would have happily allowed you to stay the night, but you see we have no spare bed.' Jonathan looked at him confused. If he was not allowing him to stay, then why bring him all the way out here?

'You see the door opposite?' Samuel continued, 'that is the residence of Monsieur and Madame Lesieur. Their apartment is much larger than ours and they often rent out a spare room to those who need it.'

'That is all good and well, but there is a slight problem,' Jonathan said with embarrassment creeping into his face. 'For you see I have no money with which to pay these people.' Samuel strode past Jonathan and knocked loudly against the chunky wooden door.

Seconds passed and finally an elderly woman answered the door, clearly in her late seventies. She gave a warm smile upon seeing Samuel at her doorstep. Her face was warm and rosy-cheeked, while her dark greying hair was perfectly straight and tied up into a bun that sat on top of her head. She had large oval shaped glasses that magnified her green eyes, and the grey apron she wore was covered in flour.

'Is everything okay?' She looked at Samuel with concern upon seeing Jonathan standing helplessly. Samuel spoke to Madame Lesieur quietly and quickly - Jonathan struggled to make out anything that was said. He did however catch a brief description of his attempt to jump into the river. Jonathan cringed as he felt his cheeks redden. Finally, Madame Lesieur looked past Samuel and gave Jonathan a warm smile.

'Please Sir, come in.' She held out both her hands. Jonathan gave a small smile. 'Now, you are just in time as I was about to prepare dinner.' She squeezed on Jonathan's hand and ushered him through the doorway. 'Good night Samuel,' she called back. 'Please send my regards to Sophia.'

'Good night Anne, and a pleasure to meet you Jonathan,' Samuel called out before turning towards his own apartment.

'Thank you.' Jonathan managed to call back to Samuel before the door was shut again.

Once inside the apartment Jonathan barely had time to take in the small sitting room as he was marched straight through it and along the slender corridor into one of the bedrooms.

'Now this should do you nicely – the bathroom is at the end of the corridor, and spare blankets and towels can be found in the chest of drawers next to the window. I will be in the kitchen if you need me, and my husband will be home shortly, so we will have formal introductions then.' She gave another warm smile before showing herself out of the room.

'Thank you, Madame Lesieur.' Jonathan called after her as she closed the door. The door flew back open and in popped her head once more.

'You can call me Anne, and my husband is called Olivier, but you best wait to be given permission from him before you call him that; you wouldn't want to be rude.' She let out a high-pitched squawk of a laugh before slamming the door firmly behind her, causing the wall to vibrate slightly.

Jonathan stood motionless in the unfamiliar bedroom, unsure of what to do with himself. It was a plain room with a simple double bed, one bedside cupboard and a three-set drawer beside the window. Jonathan noticed a newspaper lying upon the drawers, Anne had brought it through from the sitting room and left it for him. Without even picking it up, he scanned for the date along the top. June 30th 1889.

For once in his life, Jonathan was speechless.

Chapter THREE

A loud banging on the door caused Jonathan to wake. 'Where am I?' He whispered, his voice croaky. His eyes took a second to adjust to his surroundings.

'It's just me dear; dinner will be served in ten minutes.' Jonathan listened as footsteps from beyond the door scuttled away. He sat up and scanned the room; he had only intended to lay on the bed for a moment, but must have fallen asleep. The likelihood of this still being a dream was beginning to wear thin, and a sickening feeling hit Jonathan so suddenly that for a moment he thought he was going to physically vomit.

Jonathan leapt off the bed and pushed aside an opaque drape that did very little to hide the tall window behind it. He could see a small balcony, barely two feet wide, filled with a variety of flowers and shrubs in pots. It was dark out now and the small green area across the road could barely be seen, illuminated only by a small street lamp that had a lit candle within. Jonathan rubbed his forehead as he tried to make sense of where he was and how he had gotten here. He went over what he knew so far, thinking back to how he'd been waiting for Paul to collect him and drive him to the church. 'And now I am in Paris.' He spoke aloud to himself, all the while staring out at the starry sky above. 'And it would appear that the year is 1889. But how on Earth…' An overwhelming fear overcame him. 'How am I going to get home?' His thoughts returned to the carousel, his mind filled with the images of its lights blinding him, it spinning faster and faster.

'I need to get back to the carousel.'

Jonathan prised open the bedroom door and peeked through the narrow gap to see if anybody was around. He felt uncomfortable being in somebody else's home – he had never even enjoyed staying over at his own friends' and family's houses. He snuck out onto the landing.

'Oh there you are dear,' Anne called along the corridor to him, 'The bathroom is the last one on the right if you are wishing to freshen up before dinner. I'm just about to serve up.' And she spun on the spot and disappeared once more.

Jonathan did visit the bathroom briefly, and was shocked again by the sheer simplicity of it. The room was small with a large metal tub in the corner, while the toilet was a circular ceramic pot that sat against a wall. A wooden lid covered the bowl and was attached with large hinges. Finally, the sink was wooden with one long singular tap. The water it produced was strangely discoloured, and was icy cold. Jonathan all of a sudden burst into laughter.

He left the bathroom and followed the narrow corridor back towards the sitting room. There was a small wood-burning stove that was currently lifeless; above this the entire wall was overtaken with a large wooden panel, with carved decorative shelves and a large mirror. Two flowery armchairs were positioned adjacent to one and other next to the fire and opposite the fire was a small sofa, patterned like the chairs and, by the looks of it, just as uncomfortable. Jonathan was amazed by this room, with its only window being of narrow frosted glass that Jonathan predicted only looked out towards the courtyard or a neighbour. A tall lamp stood next to one of the chairs, with tassels hung from the dull green shade; a green rug lay between the chairs matching it perfectly.

Jonathan could hear voices coming from the next room. He recognised Anne's immediately, but the other voice was new; he predicted it to be that of her husband, Mister Lesieur. He entered the next room and was instantly overwhelmed by the sheer size of it. A large wooden dining room table and six chairs sat before yet another tall window that overlooked the green square outside, a cream table cloth sitting perfectly on top with two small silver candlestick holders in the middle, a single lit candle burning within each one. Three plates and sets of cutlery were set out with perfect precision, and a small glass vase filled with delicate purple flowers sat between the candles in the middle of the table. The ceilings in the apartment were high, something especially noticeable in the dining room due to a large chandelier with its bronze frame and sparkling glass that twinkled against the light of the eight candles mounted upon its outstretched metal arms.

'There you are dear.' Anne suddenly appeared through a very narrow doorway carrying three large wine glasses between her fingers. In her other hand she held a large bottle of wine. She placed them on the table gently before turning back to the door. 'Take a seat, pour the wine,' she called out to Jonathan in a cheery tone before disappearing yet again. Jonathan did as he was told and sat down in one of the seats; the bottle of wine was already open.

'Now you must be our guest for the evening,' came the deep voice of a man. Jonathan jumped up. In entered a tall slender gentleman with thick combed-back white hair and a large white bushy moustache that connected to even bigger sideburns. Jonathan didn't know whether to stand or stay seated to great this suited gentleman.

'Yes, Monsieur Lesieur,' Jonathan said in a timid voice, 'I am very grateful to you and your wife and hope this unplanned stay will not be too much trouble for you.'

'Trouble?' Monsieur Lesieur bellowed with a laugh, 'My boy, my wife will be disappointed if it is only for the one night. If it was up to her our home would be run as a boarding-house.' Monsieur Lesieur took his seat at the head of the table and sipped from his glass of wine – Jonathan thought it looked tiny clenched in his giant hands. In came Madam Lesieur carrying a large circular dish.

'I hope you like pie,' she said in her soft tone.

'Of course he likes pie,' Monsieur Lesieur interrupted, 'the man could do with a good meal inside of him, look how thin he is.'

'Thank you Madam and Monsieur Lesieur.'

'Now what have I told you lad, call me Anne.'

'Yes, and I am Olivier,' Monsieur Lesieur said, holding out his hand to shake Jonathan's. 'I apologies I did not introduce myself. And what is your name?'

'I'm Jonathan Snow.'

'British?' Questioned Olivier

'Yes sir.' Jonathan felt himself blush.

'And what brings you to Paris, Jonathan?'

Olivier continued as his wife began serving the pie, 'are you planning to visit the new tower whilst here?'

'New tower?' Jonathan questioned.

'You know, the one down at the Exposition Universelle.' Jonathan looked at Olivier with utter confusion.

'I'm sorry, but what exactly is the Exposition Universelle?' he asked, tucking into the steaming hot pie now before him. Olivier nearly spat out his wine.

'What do you mean what is the Exposition Universelle? Is he joking with me Anne? Surely you have heard of the world fair boy?' Jonathan looked sheepish. He stayed quiet.

'Darling, please,' Anne interjected, 'Jonathan does not need a lecture.'

'But Anne, I am merely shocked that this man has not heard of the great Eiffel tower.'

'Oh, that tower,' Jonathan interrupted, 'I'm sorry, yes I have heard of that one, I saw it earlier today. I didn't think of it as new.'

'Well young man, it did only open three months ago, and it is the centre piece of the fair.' Olivier sat up taller in his chair. Jonathan was about to ask if he'd had any involvement with it, but before he could speak Olivier jumped in. 'I am one of the directors of the Paris fair. It has been over twenty years since France hosted the Exposition Universelle, and this year is already proving to be not only our best, but one of the best world fairs anywhere. The tower has been an enormous success, and if I am honest I will be sad to see it torn down.'

'Torn down?' Jonathan gasped. 'Why would they take it down?'

'Unfortunately son, Gustave Eiffel has only a twenty year permit for the tower. After that it is to be taken down. Twenty years is still a good amount of time, but personally I think it should stay; it is, after all, the tallest man-made structure in the world, and to many people a new vision for the future of Paris.'

Jonathan smiled. 'I wouldn't worry too much if I were you.'

'Why?'

'Just a hunch.'

After dinner Olivier retired to the sitting room with a book and perched himself in front of the wood burner, which he had lit to take away the slight chill in the air. Anne refused his help with the dishes, so Jonathan decided to take himself back to his room. His watch had stopped working ever since he'd arrived in Paris, so he wasn't sure of the time; nonetheless he was exhausted and wouldn't turn away the chance of an early night.

'Olivier,' Jonathan interrupted his reading as he passed through the sitting room, 'will you be going to the tower tomorrow?'

'Of course, weekends are our busiest days you know.'

'Would you be able to show me the way, I was hoping to get back to that area.' Jonathan knew that if he was ever going to get home he would need to get back to the carousel.

'That'll be no problem lad,' Olivier said, before swiftly holding his book back up to his face.

Jonathan returned to his bedroom, more optimistic this time. He had enjoyed his brief time in 1889 Paris, but it was time to go home.

Chapter FOUR

The night was long and Jonathan barely slept, despite his exhaustion. His mind had so many different thoughts rushing through at once and he could barely keep up. With everything that had happened since arriving in Paris, it was only now his thoughts returned to his wedding. Why had Nicola not shown up to the church? Jonathan racked his brain to think of a reason, blaming himself and trying to think what he could have possibly done. He then wondered if time was continuing without him, and if so how long it would be before he was missed; he knew his parents would be beside themselves with worry.

The thick felt curtains that covered the large windows and concealed the darkness outside began to display light around the edges, letting slip that a new day was about to begin.

It wasn't long after this that Jonathan heard Anne talking in a hushed tone to her husband in the small corridor outside his room. Jonathan tried to listen but could not make out her words; finally both pairs of footsteps could be heard walking past the door and away towards the dining room.

Jonathan dressed and left the confines of his room. He found Anne and Olivier at the dining room table drinking coffee.

'Good morning,' Anne said, standing instantly. 'Please sit down; I will pour you a cup of coffee.' And before Jonathan could say a word she dashed past him and away to the kitchen, reappearing seconds later with an empty cup. She poured coffee from a small silver pot that was engraved with decorative scrolls and a coat of arms. She passed Jonathan the cup and placed the pot back onto a large silver tray engraved with the same pattern. The tray also held a larger pot with hot steam escaping from the spout, a round sugar bowl and a delicate little pear-shaped jug with what looked to be cream inside.

Jonathan sat and sipped his coffee from the small bone china cup and saucer, after saying good morning and telling Anne he slept well, which of course was a lie. After that he was unsure how to proceed with regular conversation; he didn't really know them, and they of course did not know him. Anne and Olivier clearly felt the same as they sat in silence drinking their coffee; it was obvious in Anne's face that she was trying to think of a conversation starter. She fiddled with her coffee cup.

'Have you no jacket, Jonathan? Or a spare shirt?' Anne asked, breaking the silence.

'No,' answered Jonathan sheepishly, 'I arrived in Paris quite unexpectedly; I didn't expect to need an overnight bag.' It was the truth, and as far as Jonathan dared go into the details of his arrival.

'It is to be a warm day; a jacket shouldn't be essential, but please let me offer you a clean shirt from my husband's closet.' Anne was already on her feet before she had finished speaking.

'Please do not go to any trouble Madam Lesieur, once I get back to the tower area I will be able to make my way home. You have done enough for me already.' Anne gave him a displeased look, but refrained from arguing and sat back down.

'Are you ready to set off soon, lad?' Olivier cut in, rising to his feet.

'Yes, sir.' Jonathan drained his cup and stood to leave.

'Now hold on,' Anne said before racing out towards the kitchen once more, again returning in seconds and holding out her hand to Jonathan. 'I want you to take this.' And she forced something into his hand before he could stop her, even closing his palm around the item before he could refuse. Jonathan uncurled his fist to reveal four silver coins.

'No,' He said immediately, 'I will not accept this.' And he tried to hand back the coins.

'That is not my money, Jonathan,' Anne began to explain whist hiding her hands from his. 'These are the coins Samuel gave me, he wanted me to have them for your stay, however you have not been a burden to me and my husband and I would rather see them go towards helping you find your way home.'

Jonathan stood motionless for a moment. A

deep guilt overwhelmed him as the gesture struck a chord in him.

'Now go, and travel safely back to your family,' Anne continued, as she scooped Jonathan into an unexpected hug. She then turned and kissed her husband farewell, and saw them both to the door. 'And Jonathan,' Anne called from the doorway before he could descend the stairwell, 'remember you are always welcome, if you ever find yourself in Paris again in the future.' Jonathan smiled. Never had a complete stranger opened up their heart to him as she had. His smile quickly faded as he realized he'd never see Anne and Olivier again.

Jonathan trailed behind Olivier as they walked. He did not speak as he strolled down the pavement and round the corner, stopping abruptly beside a tall street lamp that still had a lit flame burning away inside. The narrow cobbled road had two thin tracks for the tram, as well as an assortment of electronic cables overhead. As Jonathan searched for something to break the silence, he was abruptly distracted by the sound of a rusty squeaking noise.

From around the corner came a young man in a respectable suit and top hat, riding a rather interesting looking tricycle. The man, who was sat between two large metal-framed wheels, that was so large they came up to Jonathan's chest. The man balanced on a small seat, and gripped thin handlebars that rested above a smaller front wheel. As he peddled past Jonathan and Olivier he called out a friendly 'Bonjour.' Olivier raised a hand in recognition, but did not respond verbally as the cyclist dashed on by. Jonathan covered his mouth with his hand to stop himself from laughing out loud. His mind filled with the image of a man riding a penny-farthing, with one oversized wheel to the front and a small one to the back, that's what kind of bicycle he envisioned seeing in this time period.

Moments later, a tram appeared, its brakes screaming from the strain and steam from the engine filling the narrow street. The tram was again crowded, but this time it seemed to be more businessmen in suits. Jonathan managed to squeeze himself onto the edge of a seat before the tram took off again along the road. Olivier did not speak for the entire journey which again took less than twenty minutes.

'Do you need me to point you in any direction?' Olivier finally spoke as they watched the tram leave them behind on the pavement. Jonathan had a brief look around; he could see the Eiffel tower only a short distance away.

'I should be okay from here. Thank you again for you hospitality and please thank your wife again for me.' He shook Olivier's hand as he spoke, a sadness in his tone as he said goodbye.

'Well you know how to find us if you need a bed; have a safe journey home.' And with that, Olivier turned and took off down the road in the direction of the tower. Jonathan waited a few moments before following in the same direction.

It was another clear blue day, and temperatures were already beginning to rise despite it not even being 9 o'clock. Jonathan watched Olivier as he made his way across the road and over the bridge towards the tower, before finally disappearing out of sight.

Jonathan stood for a moment, and took in the delights of the tower as well as the sounds and smells of the city. He smirked, amused to think that this was his first ever visit to Paris. The traffic was already beginning to build, but the pavements were relatively quiet. As Jonathan made his way back towards the green, he thought about the people he had met: Samuel with the handlebar moustache and his family who had kindly helped him; and of course Anne and Olivier who had taken him in as a complete stranger. He wished he could simply head home and come back again for a visit whenever he liked, but he knew that this was impossible.

Walking back across the manicured grass, Jonathan paused; the carousel was not where he had thought it would be. His stomach sunk as he began to jog along the grass, hoping that it was maybe further along through the cluster of trees than he had remembered; but the green was not very large and from it he could see straight through the lines of thin trees. The carousel was nowhere to be seen.

Chapter FIVE

The city was crowded again, with horse-drawn carriages and trams all dashing past. The noise of the hooves and the shouting of the handlers echoed through the streets, and the rattling of the trams all clanging together and racing along the streets created a music that became the backdrop of the city. Jonathan had been resting against a tree looking out towards the tower for almost an hour. His face was pale and his stomach in knots. He had already vomited from running up and down the green numerous times, hoping that he had missed the carousel somewhere amongst the large number of trees. After five circuits of the green he'd needed to sit, and found himself on the dusty ground, shaded by the row of trees.

Rubbing his forehead with his fingers, he tried to ease the headache that was beginning to cloud his thoughts. The image of his parents, of his fiancée Nicola, of his best friend Paul all flashed into his thoughts as he wondered if he was ever going to see them again.

It was another twenty minutes before Jonathan finally took his head from his clasped hands and looked up at the view before him. The Eiffel tower looked to be sparkling against the bright sunlight and all of a sudden the scene before him changed, although not physically; Jonathan saw the view before him with new eyes. Something about being in Paris excited him, and although he could not shake the worry from the back of his mind, he found he wasn't afraid anymore.

He stood, balancing himself against the trunk of the tree as he stretched his aching body. His legs were like jelly and he needed to give himself a moment before he was confident letting go of the tree.

Jonathan crossed the road and made his way

alongside the river wall and over the wide bridge towards the Eiffel tower. The number of people all heading towards it was a sight in itself, and many of the people were married couples, mostly with children. People from all different walks of life had come to visit the tower, all dressed smart in long dresses and hats, the men in suits. Jonathan felt a little out of place not having a jacket or hat himself. The atmosphere was alive with excitement; many of the people were visitors of Paris and were here solely to visit the tower, and the world fair.

As Jonathan crossed the Seine river, he saw it was not only the tower that was catching people's eyes; lining the river bank were grand buildings that stood as an elaborate entrance into the world fair beyond. Behind the smaller building to his right stood a small platform where a locomotive was stationed. Its small engine was puffing out clouds of smoke that scattered around the surrounding area, and the small carriages to the rear would, Jonathan thought, carry no more than four people sat across. It was already swarmed with people getting on and off. Stepping over the narrow tracks of the miniature train,

Jonathan continued on towards the tower where the road was lined with giant flag poles, each displaying a different country's flag.

The atmosphere at the base of the tower was electric, and the summer breeze carried along with it the joy of people's laughter as they admired the vast structure before them. Every one of them was aiming for the centre of the tower's base so they could stand and look up into its core as it loomed over them. The four enormous feet had large queues of people at them, and within the metal cobweb design Jonathan could see masses of individuals climbing the steep steps towards the first level. The thought alone of such task had Jonathan exhausted. Standing under the tower was a strangely satisfying feeling. Having never been to Paris before, he was revelling in the buzz.

Directly beyond the tower was a long narrow pond with rows of small water sprinklers spraying up crystal clear water. At the end of the pond, standing tall and taking centre stage was the most impressive water feature Jonathan had ever seen. Upon it in carved white stone were numerous bodies of children, and on the very top stood an angel, whose wings stretched out wide as though absorbing the heat from the sun. Water was being sprayed in all directions, and the sound it made as it crashed back down against the pool below was somewhat therapeutic. Around it stretched a green haven – an enormous square filled with the greenest of grass, small thin trees that had clearly been planted for the occasion, and an array of colourful flowers that filled Jonathan's view with a pallet of colour. Interspersed around the pond were red-and-white-striped canopy style tents, providing seating and shade. An array of flagpoles again lined the pathways along both sides of the pond, but this time it was only the French flag that was being displayed.

The whole area was surrounded by what looked like one continual building with tall crystal clear windows on two levels and gold decorative architecture. The building hugged the garden from both sides and at the far end of the green was a ginormous dome that towered high above the rest of the building, demanding attention. The doors to the front were wide open, and people were making their way inside; curious, Jonathan followed to see what lay within. The dome itself was impressive – it was entirely gold with a patterned decorative display climbing up towards the top, which itself bore yet another large angel. This one was much taller than the one on the fountain, and was entirely gold. In its hand it held aloft a sword. The large dome was mounted on top of the main entrance, but the entrance itself looked less like a building and more like a giant arch, with carvings that stretched from the ground up towards the dome. In the centre of the arch, which was large enough to fit a two-storey house, was the largest wall of solid glass Jonathan had even seen. It gleamed in the sun and reflected patterns that came from the fountain.

Once inside, Jonathan stopped dead in his tracks. He inhaled sharply and gazed around. He was standing in a large circular entrance foyer that was lavishly decorated with painted walls that extended right up into the dome above him, depicting people dressed in elegant clothing. Directly opposite the glass archway was a similar painted archway, this time without the glass, and as Jonathan followed the crowd of people though, he was astonished by the scale of the hall in which he now stood. The ceiling was high and mighty like an impressive train station, with huge iron beams that held together the multiple arched roofs; glass strips ran parallel to one another, which flooded the area below with natural light. The arena-style room was divided into smaller booth areas where pop-up shops and stalls stood. The shops, themselves all different shapes, sizes and colours, bustled with life as people browsed produce and haggled with shopkeepers. Some of the larger stalls where so elaborate that they had the facade of a real shop – there were doors fitted and fake windows and signs. Smaller stalls took on the appearance of carnival-style market traders, with bright colours and flags to symbolize which country they represented. There were places selling food, others selling clothing and some even selling jewellery; in fact, at every corner of the room different stalls could be found. An awestruck grin stretched itself over Jonathan's face.

'Jonathan?' A voice called from behind, causing him to jump. He turned and instantly saw Olivier trudging towards him. His large white moustache and even larger sideburns were instant eye catchers, and made him stand out against the crowd.

'What are you doing here?' He asked in an almost accusing tone. Jonathan stuttered as he searched for an answer – he knew it would have to be a lie.

'I thought I would have a look at the fair before I left town. I may not get another chance.' He hated himself for lying, but he knew the truth was out of the question. What he really needed was another place to spend the night.

'What a splendid idea son, after all, it is the best exposition Paris has ever thrown. Have you been through to the engineering room next door? It is fascinating to see all the new technology being invented around the world, and I must say that the things being created are unthinkable.' Olivier's face was lit up; he was clearly very proud of the exposition..

'Monsieur Lesieur, I wonder if I may ask you something?' Jonathan felt the nerves creeping back up through him. He didn't want to put Olivier and his wife out, and he certainly did not want them to feel pressured into taking him in, but he felt as though they were the only people in Paris that he could fully trust. Besides, he certainly didn't want to sleep rough.

'What is it lad?' Olivier looked at Jonathan with genuine concern in his face.

'It appears that the person I was hoping to help me get home is not where I expected to find them.' Jonathan's stomach churned at his own lie, but he could hardly tell him it was a carousel that had vanished. 'I was wondering if you could help me find somewhere to stay for a few nights until I can get myself organised.' Jonathan couldn't look Olivier in the eye. Hardly a second had passed when Jonathan suddenly felt the impact of Olivier's large hand slap him on the back, almost winding him.

'You will stay with us, and I will not hear any arguments from you about it.'

'But Mousier Lesieur, I do not have anything to pay you for your hospitality.'

'Jonathan, please call me Olivier. I am not offering you a place to stay for profit, I am doing so because I can see you are a genuine man who needs a helping hand. Plus if the wife knew I hadn't offered, I would be out sleeping in the stairwell tonight.' He chuckled aloud, causing his moustache to wobble. 'Have you eaten yet?' his face returned to a serious expression. Jonathan shook his head but before he could say anything Olivier had grabbed him by the elbow and began talking loudly as he led him through the hall. 'Now I am not in long today, it being a Sunday and all, so I just need to grab my briefcase and we can go. Anne will be home from church by the time we get back. But first you need to eat.' Olivier pushed Jonathan through a small doorway of one of the exhibition stands designed to look like a romantic diner. There were numerous booths lined up against the windows and a silver reflective bar with numerous alcoholic beverages stacked behind it. Olivier directed Jonathan into an empty booth, passed him a menu and strolled up to the bar where a young woman in a stripped apron and matching hat was standing. 'Good morning Sir, can I help you?' she asked.

'Yes, please make sure this gentleman is well fed and watered, I will return to collect him shortly. Please charge the bill to me.' And he showed her an identification card that Jonathan only now realised was hanging around his neck.

'Yes Sir,' the woman replied. With that, Olivier turned to leave the diner.

It was nearly half an hour before Olivier returned, in which time Jonathan had enjoyed a cold drink and a sandwich. He hadn't wanted to take advantage of Olivier's generosity, despite the waitress asking him every ten minutes if he would like something else. Upon Olivier reentering the diner, he took a seat opposite Jonathan.

'Now, you are more than welcome to stay with us for as long as you need to. But tell me this truthfully: is it simply money that is stopping you from returning back home?' Jonathan did not know how to answer. How could he explain? 'Jonathan, I'm sorry, I do not mean to pry, and your face tells me it is not about the money. If you need help with anything then please let me know.' He gave a smile, after which he gestured for them to leave.

The glare of the sun was now noticeably warmer as the morning turned to afternoon. The chairs which circled the large pond, shaded by the canopy tents, were all full as people watched another beautiful day pass by. Olivier did not speak much as they marched on past the rows of seats and directly under the Eiffel tower back towards the bridge. The river was now filled with boats of many shapes and sizes, some carrying passengers and others carrying goods. It was almost as busy as the chaotic main road that was still bursting with passing traffic.

Olivier directed them back towards the tram stop, and it wasn't long before they were again on the tightly packed metal box of a tram, hurtling down the road. Jonathan admired from his smoke-smeared window the passing traffic and pedestrians. He had seen numerous black and white pictures of the past, but being here and seeing everything in colour seemed like make-believe, as though it was not real lift.

It hadn't felt as though he had been on the tram for very long when Olivier tugged at his arm. The tram stopped abruptly and they were once again standing up the narrow street they had been on only that morning. As they turned the corner onto Olivier and Anne's street, they saw unlocking the door to the apartment block was Samuel and his wife Sophia, with their young son Frédéric. They spotted Olivier and Jonathan approaching and held the door until they caught up.

'Good afternoon Monsieur Lesieur,' Samuel smiled as they passed him in the doorway, 'And good afternoon to you too Jonathan – do pardon me, I have rudely forgotten your surname,' he said.

'It is Snow, Jonathan Snow, but please – just Jonathan is enough.'

'I did not expect to see you again Jonathan,' Samuel said as he bolted the door behind them all. 'Madame Lesieur's cooking must be even better than I remember.' He laughed, the sound echoing up the stairwell, and his laughter was joined by Olivier's.

'Jonathan will be staying with us for a few days whilst he gets his affairs together,' Olivier interrupted before Jonathan could say anything. 'In fact, I was hoping to speak with you Samuel – do you have a moment?' By now they had already reached the floor of the apartments and Samuel's family were already inside.

'Of course, what is it you wished to discuss?'

'You are still working at the train station, correct?' Olivier quizzed, 'In the engineering warehouse?'

'Yes,' Samuel said, confusion written across his face.

'Are they still looking for labours? I recall you mentioning how shorthanded you are down there.'

'Oh yes Sir, between the trains and trams we are kept busy. But I don't understand where you are going with this, Monsieur Lesieur?' Olivier smirked at Samuel and turned his gaze towards Jonathan; Samuel followed his stare and he too looked upon Jonathan. Samuel soon began to smirk as he finally realised exactly what Olivier was hinting at.

Chapter SIX

It was a couple of hours later when Jonathan sat down for dinner with Anne and Olivier. He had spent much of the afternoon in their spare bedroom feeling sorry for himself. The thought of where he was and the worry of getting home overpowered him. He felt nauseous, and had a headache that refused to go away; his racing thoughts clouding his mind refused to give him a moment's piece.

Anne and Olivier were relatively quiet over dinner, talking only occasionally between themselves. Anne would try and encourage Jonathan into the conversation, but his mind was elsewhere.

'Olivier tells me you will be joining Samuel at the warehouse tomorrow. That will be a good way to earn some money; you can save it to pay for your return journey home if that's what your plans are.' Jonathan paused and looked at Anne through sad eyes; he had no home to go to, not without the help of the carousel anyway.

'I think I will take one day at a time for now; I may end up being in Paris longer than I had originally thought. But please, once I have some money behind me I will look for alternative lodgings, I understand this is only temporary.'

'Oh Jonathan dear, don't you think about that just yet. We are happy for you to stay as long as necessary.' Anne tapped him on the hand. 'Oh by the way,' she said whilst rising from the table. 'Samuel called again whilst you were resting this afternoon and has dropped off some clean shirts and trousers for you. I think you will be of a similar size and they will do you until you can buy some of your own.'

Jonathan remained quiet; he was already embarrassed by his neediness, and to be handed another man's clothes was almost beyond devastating. He had always prided himself on being so independent and responsible, and had been raised to work for the things he wanted. He quickly excused himself from the dining room table, took the sack of clothing and headed back to his room, trying his hardest to fight back tears until he was out of sight.

***

A gentle knock on the door woke Jonathan from his sleep. He was laid on top of the double bed still in his clothes.

'Good morning.' Anne's low voice came through the closed door. 'Samuel will be here in fifteen minutes to collect you, would you like anything to eat before you leave? I have a pot of coffee ready.' Jonathan sighed as he sat up on the bed.

'No thank you Anne, I will be through for some coffee.' Jonathan stretched and rubbed his eyes before finally getting off the bed. He didn't really want to get a job here, but he knew that if he was stuck in 1889 Paris, he would need money to pay Anne and Olivier for their generosity.

He began searching through the sack of clothes brought by Samuel, and shook his head in disbelief. Inside were three shirts: a white one, a pale blue, and a grey and white stripped one; there were also three sets of trousers, two black and one grey; finally at the bottom of the sack was a large dark blue, slightly worn set of overalls that were comparable to dungarees. He quickly changed into a fresh set of trousers and put on the pale blue shirt; he still had on his black shoes from the wedding, which seemed a tad over the top for a day in an engine workshop, but it was all he had.

Taking the overalls with him, Jonathan left his room and found Anne and Olivier at the dining room table drinking coffee. A smile filled Anne's face as he entered the room wearing his newly acquired clothing. 'They are a good fit – I knew Samuel would be a similar size to you. He will be here any minute, so make sure to drink your coffee.' A large mug had already been poured for Jonathan. Taking the seat opposite Anne, he quickly downed the lukewarm coffee.

'Where is it exactly Samuel works?' Jonathan asked, still trying to wake up.

'Well,' Olivier spoke, clearing his throat as though ready to start a long speech, 'Samuel works at

Gare du Nord, the largest train station in France, and with the extension it is currently undergoing it is expected to be one of the largest in the world. Did you know –' He was interrupted by a loud knock on the front door. Jonathan breathed an inward sigh of relief. Anne jumped up and left the dining room to answer the door, and Jonathan quickly followed before Olivier could continue his rambling.

'Ah good morning Samuel,' Anne spoke in a high-pitched voice, 'please, come in.'

'Thank you Madame Lesieur, but I was simply wanted to check if Jonathan was ready to leave.' Jonathan came into view of the doorway, and he spotted that Samuel was already wearing his overalls.

'Just give me a moment to slip into these,' Jonathan said, 'I am afraid I only have these shoes, will they be okay?' Samuel looked down and saw Jonathan's black polished shoes and began to laugh.

'Don't worry; we have spare boots at the warehouse. I am pleased to see the clothes fit.'

'Thank you for lending me them, I'll make sure to return them as soon as I get my own.' Jonathan tried his best not to let his embarrassment show.

Upon leaving the apartment, Anne took hold of Jonathan and gave him the tightest of hugs. Slightly winded, Jonathan thanked her again for taking him in and wished her a good day, before following Samuel down the stairwell and back out onto the street.

It was yet another blue sky, and the morning mist was still visible across the small green adjacent to the apartment building. Samuel had with him a leather bag, and wore the same dark blue overalls as Jonathan. Despite his tatty looking work clothing, he still took care of his appearance, with his short black hair perfectly slicked back and his characteristic handlebar moustache perfectly oiled above his constant smile. He was very talkative this morning, and spoke to Jonathan as though they were old friends.

Jonathan expected them to wait at the tram stop, but he marched straight past it onto a much larger street. Here the traffic was already building, and trams could be seen hurtling in all directions. The noise of this busy street was the first thing to hit Jonathan; the trams' electrical sound fizzed and pedestrians, mostly men in suits, all rushed past Jonathan and Samuel to catch a tram headed in the opposite direction.

'Quickly,' Samuel shouted back to Jonathan before taking off at speed. Jonathan wasn't sure why they were now running but pursued Samuel nonetheless. It didn't take long for Jonathan to figure out why they were in a hurry; Samuel was aiming for a tram that had stopped to pick up passengers and was getting ready to leave. With only metres to go, the tram began to move, but Samuel didn't stop his pursuit; charging for the tram, he took hold of the rear handle and pulled himself aboard before it could build up enough speed. He looked back at the bewildered Jonathan, his hair blowing in the wind. Samuel reached out his hand to Jonathan, but the tram was continuing to gain speed faster than Jonathan could run. With a final push, Jonathan gave his all and managed to grab hold of Samuel's hand, who instantly pulled him forward and onto the back of the tram.

'We need to get you better shoes,' Samuel sniggered.

The tram eventually terminated in a large train station. The platforms were filled with several trams and hundreds of pedestrians all racing past one another.

'This way,' Samuel gestured forward, already zig-zagging his way through the crowds of people. Jonathan followed him around the edge of the tram station and through a doorway that led into an even larger station, this one filled with large steam trains puffing out clouds of smoke that filled the platforms. Jonathan wanted to stop and take in this colossal building; it again was filled with hundreds of people all hurrying to catch their trains or heading out to the trams and city. An announcement was made over the end of one of the platforms, by a man who stood on a raised platform. He shouted loud above the crowd announcing that the train was about to leave.

'Mesdames et Messieurs, le train pour Bruxelles est sur le point de partir à la plate-forme de douze.' The voice of the man spoke so quickly that Jonathan struggled to make out exactly what had been said. He suddenly wondered whether Anne, Olivier and Samuel had been speaking slower to help him understand them. At the far end of the station Samuel finally stopped at a pair of metal double doors. He pushed one aside and gestured for Jonathan to go in ahead.

Inside, with the metal door closed back into position, the noise of the rowdy station was dimmed. Jonathan now stood in what looked like a cross between a smaller station and a warehouse, with tracks coming in from a large opening in the far wall. Beyond were five steam engines arranged in a perfect line, and beyond those were three trams. The engines were positioned over holes in the ground that Jonathan instantly recognised as working areas.

'Stay here.' Samuel raised a hand and took off towards a small office in the corner of the large warehouse. A window facing out towards the workspace let Jonathan see Samuel as he entered and began speaking to an older man sat behind a desk. The man, who was, Jonathan guessed, in his late fifties, instantly looked over Samuel's shoulder and out of the glass window in the direction of Jonathan. He did not speak but continued to stare as Samuel spoke. Jonathan felt himself redden and he shifted on his feet, trying to avoid the man's gaze. Finally Samuel stopped talking and waited for the man to respond, he did not look at Samuel, nor did he speak, but instead raised a fist in front of him and, raising his index finger, gestured towards Jonathan to come in. With every step Jonathan felt more and more nervous – this man was clearly in charge, and he didn't want to do anything foolish.

'Samuel tells me you are looking for work.' The man's voice was hoarse, as though he struggled to breath. He was round in figure, with a thick auburn beard that was going grey, and a receding hairline to match.

'Yes Sir.'

'Samuel has given me his word that he will be responsible for you, so I am happy for you to begin immediately. Samuel will show you the ropes, and make sure you have everything you need. You will be paid weekly and if you give me any doubts at all I will throw you out faster than you can say arc de triomphe. Do I make myself clear?'

'Yes Sir.' Samuel turned to leave the office,

and Jonathan did not wait to be asked to follow.

'He is quite scary,' Jonathan said to Samuel as they made their way across the warehouse floor.

'Yes, he can be until you get to know him,' Samuel replied with a smirk.

'Have you worked here long?' asked Jonathan.

'Since I left school. The scary man in the office is my father.' Jonathan's stomach sunk and he bit his tongue. 'Let's get you some better boots and we can get going.'

As Samuel searched through an old locker, the metal doors to the warehouse opened with a loud screech and the noise of the station beyond filed the room. Two men, both in their late twenties or early thirties, entered the warehouse; they both wore the same dark blue overalls as Samuel.

'Morning Samuel,' said a man with a large muscular frame and blonde hair that was cut short, 'Who is this?' he asked, gesturing towards Jonathan.

'Lyle, this is Jonathan, he will be working here now.' Lyle took as step forward and grabbed Jonathan's hand into his own for a tight handshake.

'Pleased to meet you Jonathan, don't let

Samuel boss you around.' He let out a deep laugh, released Jonathan's hand and walked away to his own locker. The other man stood there, waiting to be introduced. He was a lot thinner than Lyle, had round thick-framed glasses and the curliest hair Jonathan had ever seen on a man.

'Jonathan, this is René,' Samuel said. René was less forward when it came to introductions and kept his hands firmly to his side.

'Nice to meet you Jonathan,' he said in a whisper of a voice, 'I hope you settle in well.' Satisfied with his introduction, René turned and left. Jonathan found the two men amusing; they could not have been any different if they had tried.

'Aha!' Samuel called out, shocking Jonathan out of his thoughts. 'I knew there were spare boots in here somewhere. Here, try these on.' He threw a dirty old pair of boots on the floor. Jonathan didn't waste any time removing his now dusty and grazed wedding shoes, and crouched down to try on the boots. They were a little big, but they would do.

Jonathan spent the entire day with Samuel,

who talked him through the various tasks he performed on a regular basis.

'So the two engines to the left are here for servicing. They are full of rust, soot and all kind of rubbish that is causing them problems, so it is our job to clean them up and send them back out. The other two engines no longer work, so again it is our job to figure out what is wrong and get them fixed up as soon as possible. As for the two trams, they are knackered and need scrapping, but we have been asked to repair them in the hope they will be back in service soon.' Jonathan found the whole thing strangely interesting.

'I didn't tell you before, but back home I'm a mechanic. But I work mostly with cars and...' he paused abruptly, forgetting himself and where he was. Samuel looked with genuine interest. '...but it will all be very different on trains and trains I guess.'

'Most engines are the same, just a different size. I think you will pick things up quickly.' Said Samuel.

Jonathan watched Lyle service the two locomotives, both of which he'd finished by the end of the day. His large frame and muscular body meant that he rarely struggled with heavy pieces of equipment, and thus he was often given the heavy lifting jobs. René appeared to be more of a problem solver and worked on one of the other locomotives, trying to figure out what was wrong with it. Samuel took charge of the trams, taking them apart, replacing various pieces and giving them a clean. Jonathan spent most of the morning taking in what they were all doing, as well as fetching and carrying tools and parts when called upon. René even shouted Jonathan over when he had found the locomotive's problem to show it to him.

'Do you see that?' He asked Jonathan, pointing into the engine at nothing specific.

'Oh yes,' replied Jonathan, 'the cylinder is cracked, and the supporting bar has rusted over so much its causing the brakes to struggle. And is that a hairline crack in the tank'

'Bloody hell,' gasped René, 'I hadn't even seen the crack.' René scratched his head. 'I don't think I need to teach you too much.'

The day itself passed by quickly, and Jonathan

spent the remainder of the afternoon helping Samuel dismantle a tram engine.

'Have you done this before?' He asked, watching Jonathan confidently strip down the grease covered machinery.

'Not on a tram,' smiled Jonathan, 'but these engines are fairly simple. I can see this is the one that only needs to be cleaned up, as everything seems to be in working condition.' Just then a siren called out through the workshop and Samuel dropped his tools.

'Home time,' he said with a broad smile. 'Time to go.'

Chapter SEVEN

The journey back to the apartment seemed much longer than the trip out had, and the tram was crowded with what felt like a hundred commuters all squeezed in. Samuel had barely spoken during the ride back, but once back on the street he once again talked non-stop until they reached the apartment building's doors. He seemed more than happy to tell Jonathan about himself, and told him that he had been married to Sophia for five years, and that she'd become pregnant with their son Frédéric almost instantly. He had worked at the transport warehouse since he was fourteen years old, and they had moved into this apartment block only two years ago. Jonathan was impressed at how much information Samuel could fit into the short walk.

The draughty stairwell was poorly lit, and the two men made their way up to the second floor. As they reached their landing, Samuel wished Jonathan a pleasant evening.

'I will knock for you again in the morning. It will be the same time,' He said before unlocking his own front door and disappearing inside. Jonathan knocked on the door of Anne and Olivier, and within moments Anne opened the door. Before Jonathan could even say a word, his eyes were instantly drawn to the ground where a small dog ran from inside the apartment, its tail wagging. It proceeded to sniff at Jonathan's ankles. It was a very small wire-haired Jack Russell, with a white body and tanned face. There was a white strip running from its nose to the top of its head.

'Come now Jack, let Jonathan inside,' Anne called to the dog, and it immediately turned and ran back inside at full speed. Jonathan couldn't take his eyes from the cute little dog as it ran around the sitting room in excitement, bounding back towards him wagging its tail.

'I'm pretty certain you didn't have a dog this morning Anne,' he laughed, 'where did he come from?' Jonathan said, crouching down to the floor and making a fuss of the excitable animal.

'My granddaughter has returned from visiting family in the south, this is her dog,' Anne replied, watching Jack as he continued circling them both, his running and skipping mimicking that of a spring lamb.

'Your granddaughter?' Jonathan exclaimed.

'Yes, she has been in Toulouse for over a week. She returned this afternoon.' Anne took the lead and headed for the dining room, the little Jack Russell hot on her heels.

'Did she travel alone?' Jonathan asked, following Anne into the next room.

'This time she did, yes. Camille is nineteen years old, a young woman of the world. I thought she may have stayed out there this time as she enjoys it so much.' Anne began clearing away two cups of tea and a teapot that sat on the table. Jonathan opened his mouth to speak, but before he could ask any more questions a voice entering the room stopped him in his tracks.

'Mémé, would you like help with dinner, I...' she paused upon seeing Jonathan standing in the centre of the room. She was tall and slender, with dark hair that fell below her shoulders, and large piercing eyes that took in all of Jonathan. Her skin was not pale like her grandparents', but a smooth sun-kissed caramel.

'Camille, let me introduce you to Jonathan, the young man I was telling you about, the one that will be staying with us for a while.'

'Pleasure,' she said in a harsh tone that made Jonathan feel slightly unease. She turned her gaze back upon her grandmother. 'If you do not require help in the kitchen, Mémé, I will take Jack for a walk. The train ride was long and he has energy to burn.'

'Yes darling, take Jack. Papi will be home any minute so I can serve dinner when you get back.' With that, Camille turned and left.

'Come Jack,' she hollered over her shoulder, and Jack, who was still sniffing around Jonathan's legs, ran out of the door after her.

Jonathan returned to his room to change out of his dirty overalls, and freshened up in the bathroom before returning to the dining room. Olivier was now home and was sat at the table reading a newspaper. Anne was setting the table and talking to him about Camille, but it was clearly obvious he was only half-listening as he grunted over his paper every few seconds to acknowledge what she was saying.

'Oh Jonathan,' she said the moment he entered the room, 'please take a seat, I will be serving shortly.' She poured him a glass of wine before darting off into the kitchen.

It was another ten minutes before Camille returned with Jack. His claws could be heard against the tiled floors as he charged into the dining room, jumping up to greet Olivier and Jonathan.

'Get down you silly animal.' Olivier laughed, petting the dog before it ran off again. 'And how was your trip sweetheart?' He finally put down his paper and looked at his granddaughter. 'Is this another new dress?'

'Yes Papi, do you like it?' She twirled for him,

the smile across her face indicating her pleasure at him noticing. 'Mémé Aimée bought it for me.'

'How are the oldies, still as mad as ever?'

'They are very well Papi, they ask after you both and wish you would come to visit some time.' Camille was clearly excited about her trip, and she continued talking as she took the seat opposite Jonathan. Anne soon reappeared with a large pot. The most delicious aroma that Jonathan had ever smelt drifted into his nostrils.

'Camille was visiting her other grandparents,' Anne told Jonathan as she served him up what looked like some kind of stew.

'Mémé Aimée is hoping to visit Paris again in time to see the exposition, I was telling her all about the Eiffel tower and she does not believe how tall it is.' Jonathan sat back eating his food, listening to Camille talk about her family and the time she'd spent with them. She spoke quickly, and with excitement that caused Jonathan to struggle with parts of what she was saying. She did not once look at Jonathan, and continued to talk about her trip until they had all finished their meal. Meanwhile, Jack lay fast asleep under the table the whole time, resting his head against Jonathan's leg. He let out a quiet snore.

When the meal was over and Anne had cleared the table, refusing numerous offers of help, Camille decided she was tired after a day travelling and returned to her room to rest. Taking Jack with her, she left the room. Olivier retired to the sitting room where he clearly planned to spend the remainder of the evening, accompanied by a book and cigar. He'd often sit holding his cigars for a long time before lighting them. Anne remained in the kitchen making a pot of tea, and had ordered Jonathan to stay at the table to await a cup. Upon returning with the silver tray, she poured out two cups, handing one to Jonathan.

'Now my dear,' she said, as though readying herself for another long conversation. 'How was your day at the warehouse? With all the excitement of Camille's return I have barely had two minutes to ask.'

'I get paid at the end of the week, so I will be able to pay my way after that.'

'Don't you worry about that, we will talk

about that when the time comes.'

After talking for over half an hour about his day, the conversation soon turned to Camille.

'Has she always lived with you?' Jonathan asked, desperate not to come across as prying.

'She has lived with us ever since she was three years old,' Anne replied.

'And her parents?'

'Dead!' A stern voice came from the doorway. It was Camille, her mouth a flat line. 'They both died when I was young, and I have lived with Mémé Anne and Papi Olivier ever since. Is there anything else you wish to know about me Monsieur?' Her eyes had taken on a hard edge.

'No, I'm sorry,' Jonathan mumbled.

'Jack.' Camille called the little dog that had followed her in and had again run under the table, and within seconds he raced back and followed her from the room once more.

Chapter EIGHT

The night again felt long, and Jonathan couldn't sleep. He kept thinking about the carousel, not to mention his fiancé and family. Yet between thinking about his life back home, his thoughts also wandered into the events of the past few days. Anne and Olivier had opened up their home to him, and Samuel had helped him to find work without even questioning his abilities or character. Finally Jonathan's thoughts fell upon Camille; he had clearly made a bad impression on her, but he hoped she would mellow in time.

Morning arrived in the blink of an eye, and when Anne knocked on the door Jonathan's head was pounding and his eyes were heavy. When he finally entered the dining room, Anne and Olivier were already at the table drinking their morning coffee. Camille was there too, fixing a lead to Jack's collar.

'Good morning,' Jonathan said.

'Good morning dear,' Anne chirped in her usual happy voice. Olivier simply grunted over his cup of coffee, and Camille walked past Jonathan without even acknowledging his presence. As Camille left with Jack, Jonathan's face must have given away his dismay, as Anne was quick to speak.

'Do not let Camille upset you son, it is nothing you have done. She simply does not approve of us taking in those who need a place to stay. She thinks we are fools who let people walk over us,' She said whilst pouring him a cup of coffee. 'But don't worry, she will come around once she sees you are a good man.' Jonathan wasn't sure if this was a good thing or not – now he had to prove himself to her, and he wasn't exactly sure how.

As promised, Samuel knocked on the door, letting Jonathan know it was again time for work. With a swift goodbye to Anne and Olivier, he followed Samuel out of the building and in the direction of the trams. Jonathan spotted Camille and Jack walking around the edge of the green. For a split second they made eye contact. Jonathan gave a friendly but wary smile as he hurried to catch up with Samuel who was already some distance ahead. Camille watched the two men as they walked up the street. Despite her disapproval of this stranger in their home, she found him oddly intriguing, and there was something about him that just did not fit.

That day at the warehouse, Jonathan again played as Samuel's assistant. Lyle and René were quiet today, offering little more than a 'Good morning' between them. They continued with their work on the large locomotives. At lunch time, Jonathan sat with Samuel who was reading a newspaper. Jonathan had never been much good at reading French, and as Samuel held it up to read Jonathan tried to read the front page that faced him. When Samuel had finished with the paper he passed it to Jonathan, who took it without hesitation. He wondered if there would be a classifieds section; maybe he'd find a hint regarding the carousel.

'Are you looking for something in particular?' Samuel asked. Jonathan hesitated, his mind racing.

'I need to find somebody,' Jonathan started, pausing between words. 'A man… you see, I cannot go home unless I see him.'

'Do you know where this man lives, or what his name is?' Samuel asked.

'No.' Jonathan felt foolish; he sensed he could trust Samuel with the truth, but he dare not risk it. He smiled – the perfect cover story had come to him. 'The morning you bumped into me near the tower, I had only just arrived in Paris. In the treeline opposite was a carousel, the owner of which has something of mine that I must retrieve before I can go home.' Jonathan looked at Samuel for some kind of reaction.

'Can you not just return to the tower and speak with this man?'

'No. I returned the day after, but the carousel had gone. I don't have any idea where it may be and I don't know how I would find out.' Jonathan let out a sigh of relief; although it was not one hundred percent truthful, he knew this was as close as he was going to get.

'It will be difficult without knowing the man's name; did the carousel have a name?' Samuel asked, taking the newspaper back from Jonathan and flicking through the pages quickly, stopping on a page that listed events and attractions at the Paris exposition.

'I do recall seeing a name.' Jonathan put his head in his hands and began rubbing his forehead. He could picture the bright paintwork across the top, but the image in his mind was blurred. 'Carousel… Carousel de… Carousel La…'

'By any chance was it Le Cheval Carrousel Volant?' Samuel asked. Jonathan raised his head from his hands so quickly he became dizzy.

'Yes, but how did you know that?'

'Look here.' Samuel passed the newspaper back to Jonathan. In the bottom corner of the page, hidden beneath many larger advertisements was a small box containing only a few words.

'Fortune teller Madam Mystic returns to Paris this June, accompanied again by Le Cheval Carrousel Volant, a Parisian favourite. This is their second visit this year and it is expected not to be their last as the Exposition Universelle continues to draw in crowds.'

'But where are they now?' Jonathan looked at Samuel.

'Madam Mystic is a well-known name in France; she is always visited by queues of people wanting to know what their future has in store. My wife always insists on seeing her when she is in the city. Unfortunately, her arrival is never announced, and after a couple of days or weeks she disappears again. She appears in various towns and cities around France, but by the time you find out where, she will likely be gone again.'

'So what do you recommend I do?' Jonathan tried his hardest not to sound so desperate.

'She usually returns to Paris every couple of months. All you can do is wait for her to return; it will be in the paper in a similar advert. It's simply a waiting game.'

Chapter NINE

Jonathan continued to accompany Samuel to the engineering warehouse. As the week progressed, his responsibilities increased in number – soon he was arms-deep in the old trams. Camille continued to give Jonathan a wide birth, and spoke to him only when necessary. Anne on the other hand could not do enough for him, and fussed over Jonathan as though he was her own child. Olivier however was a complete contrast and spoke rarely, he was a lot more laid back; he would happily join Jonathan in conversation if he found it interesting, but if he didn't he could usually be found hidden behind the morning's newspaper or, in the evenings, a book.

When Friday finally arrived Jonathan was pleased, and

his thoughts and fears about the carousel, although still in his mind, were finally starting to ease and he was beginning to settle in. Samuel continued training him, and spent the morning showing Jonathan how to change the oil, and how to complete various other checks, and he was thrilled when he was told to have a go on a second tram alone.

'If you have any issues, just shout,' said Samuel before leaving Jonathan to it.

The warehouse was quiet today as both Lyle and René were out attending to a tram that had stopped working in the middle of the street, and it was nearly home time by the time they returned.

'Blasted thing,' Lyle cursed as he relayed what had happened to Samuel and Jonathan. His whole face and his blonde hair were covered in black greasy oil. 'I was under the engine taking a look and the oil tank cracked. I was bloody nearly drowned.' His voice got louder and louder as he spoke, echoing through the warehouse.

'It was your own fault, I told you to wait until I checked for any initial problems,' said René, trying to hide the smirk from his face. As Lyle cleaned his face with tissue paper, muttering and swearing under his breath as he did this, Samuel and Jonathan began packing away their tools. Before they left, Monsieur Baudin came out of the office and handed small envelopes to Lyle, René and Samuel before turning to address Jonathan.

'Jonathan, can I speak with you in my office please.' He did not wait for a response and turned immediately, walking back towards his office. Jonathan swallowed. Monsieur Baudin had barely left the office all week, and his only interaction with Jonathan so far had been when he had agreed to give him the job only five days ago.

'Please take a seat Jonathan, this won't take long.'

'Monsieur Baudin, may I again thank you for this opportunity you have given me.' Monsieur Baudin held up a hand...

'Jonathan, I have watched you from this office all week. I have also spoken with my son Samuel, and we both agree that you are a credit to this team. I agreed to give you a trial and I am pleased to say I am happy for you to continue here.' He passed Jonathan an envelope containing his week's wages. 'Keep up the good work son, and I will see you bright and early Monday morning. Now get out of my office.' Jonathan quickly stood and headed for the door, a smile slowly creeping across his face as he walked across the warehouse floor towards Samuel who was still waiting for him.

'Ready to leave?' he asked.

'Yes,' Jonathan replied, tucking the envelope into his pocket. As they made their way back home, Samuel noticed that Jonathan was still smiling to himself.

'You are happy to be keeping your job?' he asked.

'Yes, it is one less thing to worry about. At least now I can give Anne and Olivier something each week for my being there. I also need to pay you for the clothes you gave me.'

'Don't bother,' Samuel cut in, 'they were mostly unworn by me anyway, keep them.'

Back at the apartment, Jonathan was instantly greeted by Jack, the small rough haired Jack Russell.

He was jumping up with sheer excitement as Jonathan tried his hardest to get through the door.

'Good evening Jonathan.' Anne and Camille were at the dining room table; Anne instantly rose to her feet to embrace Jonathan as he walked into the room. 'Now come on Jack, let Jonathan in you silly dog.'

'I was paid today,' Jonathan said as he took out the envelope containing his wage, 'and Monsieur Baudin has told me that my trial is over and I am now fully hired.'

'Congratulations Jonathan,' Anne said, clapping her hands. She embraced him again into another rib-cracking hug.

'Here.' Jonathan handed Anne the envelope containing his wage. He didn't fully understand the French currency anyway, so he hoped she would take as much as she needed.

'Oh Jonathan, I do not want it all. Now, let me show you.' She emptied the contents of the envelope onto the table. Camille, who was staying quiet, kept a close eye on the proceedings.

'Now, you see these two coins?' Anne placed

two large coins into the palm of her hand and held them up to Jonathan, 'this is what I will take each week, and the rest you can use to buy yourself new clothes and save up for your travel home.' She placed the two coins in the small pocket of her apron and re-joined Camille at the table where they were both nursing cups of tea. Jonathan looked at the money left on the table. There were four silver coins, two large two small, and one large gold coin.

'Are you sure that is enough for me to give you?' Jonathan had always had a reputation for worrying not to take people for granted, and he the thought he was not giving Anne enough after all she had done was plain to see.

Camille looked up from her tea. She stared at Jonathan in a way she had not before, and a smile appeared as she silently continued to drink her tea.

'Of course Jonathan, these two coins are more than enough. Now get yourself cleaned up for dinner; Olivier will be home soon and I will be serving as soon as he arrives.' Without hesitation, Jonathan scooped the remaining coins back into the envelope and headed out of the dining room towards his bedroom.

It didn't take long for Jonathan to change into clean clothing, and after freshening up in the bathroom he headed back to the dining room, where Olivier's voice could now be heard. As Jonathan made his way along the landing, he ran straight into Camille who was coming out of her bedroom, Jack running between them both at full speed in the direction of the dining room.

'I'm sorry,' said Jonathan as he stepped back to allow Camille to pass. She looked at him cautiously, but a smile was edging into the corners of her mouth.

'No, it is I who should be sorry; Jack forgets to look where he is going sometimes in all his excitement.' For a spilt-second they stood in silence, yet it was not uncomfortable. 'I have to say, I was impressed with your generosity earlier. Many people would not have offered more money like you did.'

'Well your grandparents have been very kind to me. I cannot thank them enough for allowing me to stay. I just wish I could do more.' She finally let her smile escape before she turned to follow Jack.

Jonathan hesitated for a moment; he felt a small accomplishment in finally getting Camille's approval.

For the first time that week, Camille was talkative over dinner, and even looked at Jonathan occasionally as though involving him in the conversation.

'Madam Caballé is taking her first trip in nearly ten years, and has asked me to be in charge while she is away. I am honoured that she trusts me enough, especially with it being one of our busiest times.' Jonathan wasn't quite sure what she was talking about, but the excitement upon her face made it clear it was important to her.

'May I ask what it is you do?' Jonathan enquired, feeling brave enough to ask her without getting scowled at; and Camille replied without hesitation: 'I work at Galarie 24. The owner, Madame Caballé, has been hosting art shows there for nearly forty years. I started working there a little over a year ago and this is her first vacation in a very long time.'

'Camille, we are so proud of you.' Anne interrupted as she began to clear away dishes. 'When is Madam Caballé leaving?'

'It will be for a week in September, she is not sure which week yet as she is making arrangements to see her sister who lives in Copenhagen.' Camille began helping clear away the remaining dishes. Olivier lit a pipe and took hold of the newspaper resting on a spare chair.

'Olivier?' Jonathan interrupted, 'Do you know where I may find some clothes shops? All I have are these of Samuels and I think, now that I have a little money, I should buy some of my own.' Olivier put down the paper and looked at Jonathan, his lips pursed together as his face turned serious.

'Camille,' he said as his granddaughter walked back into the room with a large pot of tea, 'do you know if the men's tailor is still open near your gallery?'

'Yes Papi, they are open all days but Sunday. Why do you ask?'

'Young Jonathan here is in need of his own clothing, and I think Monsieur Moreau would see that he is fitted with a new set of trousers and shirts. Would you mind showing him the way tomorrow on your way to the gallery?' There was an awkward pause as Camille's eyes darted to Jonathan.

'Of course,' she said before dashing back into the kitchen.

Chapter TEN

The next morning Camille knocked on Jonathan's bedroom door at seven o' clock.

'I will be leaving in thirty minutes if you still want me to take you to the tailor,' she shouted through the closed door. Jonathan managed to holler back a sleepy 'Yes' before he heard her footsteps as she walked away.

Jonathan found Camille at the front door waiting for him. Jack was sat at her feet yawning as Jonathan finally entered the sitting room. 'I'm sorry,' He said before following her out of the door. The journey to Galarie 24 was taken by tram, and they got off directly opposite the Arc de Triomphe, another landmark Jonathan had never before seen outside of photographs. It was enormously busy, and the large arch stood as the centre of all the turmoil. Hundreds of horse-drawn carriages raced around before bearing off onto different streets leading off from the Arc, itself like a giant bee hive attracting all types of transport that circled it in a never-ending cycle of commotion. Camille had already taken off down the street and Jonathan squeezed his way through crowds of people to catch her up. She cut between two buildings, a closed pub on one side and a bank on the other; the passage was barely wide enough for two people to pass, yet Camille marched on through without looking back once. At the end of the passage they emerged back onto another large street, which again led back towards the Arc de Triomphe. Camille turned in the opposite direction and continued with speed along the pavement. As Jonathan tried to think of something to say, Camille's voice cut in.

'This is it.' She pointed at a grand wooden doorway that sat quite ambiguous against the street, the building not too dissimilar to the apartment block Camille and Jonathan lived in. Camille pressed a small buzzer next to the door, and moments later a man appeared in the doorway. He was extremely tall and thin, about forty years old, and wore a waist coat; he smiled the moment his eyes fell upon Camille.

'Ah, how are you Mademoiselle, it was only last week I was talking with Madame Caballé. Please come on in, how can I help?' He brought them into a large foyer, with marble flooring and a chandelier above them which chimed in the breeze that came through the doorway.

'Monsieur Moreau, this is Jonathan Snow, he is… well… a friend of my grandparents' and has been staying with us this past week.' Monsieur Moreau looked Jonathan up and down before extending a hand. 'He is in need of some clothing as he has arrived in Paris with nothing. May I leave him with you? I am due to be in work this morning.'

'Of course Mademoiselle, you leave him with me and I will make sure he has everything he needs. Will you be back later to collect him?' Camille again hesitated.

'Yes. I will collect him at lunchtime; I should be able to finish by then.' With that she let herself out.

'So, Monsieur Snow, please follow me and we can begin.' Monsieur Moreau took Jonathan into a large open room that was double the size of the large foyer. Against the back wall stood two rows of mannequins with various shirts and jackets upon them. In the centre of the room was a large triple-fronted mirror with a small raised area in front of it. 'Now, if you could please stand on here, I will take your measurements.' Jonathan did not speak, and stood on the platform. Monsieur Moreau began measuring Jonathan's waist, legs, arms, chest and neck. It occurred to Jonathan that he did not write anything down as he went along.

'I have a small number of items that would fit you already; they were made for somebody who decided he did not want them after all. Let us see how they look.' Monsieur Moreau brought out two pairs of trousers, two short-sleeved shirts, one long-sleeved shirt and a smart jacket. Monsieur Moreau was more hands-on than Jonathan was comfortable with, and was more than willing to help him in and out of the trousers. Jonathan did not wish to come across as rude, and said nothing as the tailor took charge, lifting

Jonathan's legs in and even fastening the zip. Finally, he ran a finger round the waistband to see how much room Jonathan had to breathe; Jonathan could sense himself standing rigid as this man continued to dress him like one of his mannequins. It didn't take Jonathan long to try them all on, and besides the trousers being slightly longer than necessary, they were all a good fit.

'I can take the trousers up in no time. You will still have everything to go by lunchtime.'

'May I enquire as to the price of these items?' Jonathan was worried that the handful of coins in his pocket was not going to be enough. He pulled them out of his pocket and showed them to Monsieur Moreau. 'This is all I have on me,' he said, slightly embarrassed.

Monsieur Moreau leaned in to look at the coins; in his hand Jonathan held four silver coins and one large gold coin. Monsieur Moreau took the gold coin and one silver.

'This will be enough for the clothing.' And he took away the trousers to a small desk sat against a window, a sewing machine on top, and began making the adjustments.

The clothing adjustments were finished long before Camille would be back, and without knowing where to go or what to do, Jonathan stayed with Monsieur Moreau, who seemed more than happy to have somebody to talk to. Jonathan was asked very little about himself and spent the majority of the conversation listening to Monsieur Moreau who liked nothing more than to retell stories of clients, and the amusing incidents that he has witnessed. At just after midday, the doorbell rang and Camille again stood in the doorway, a basket in her hands.

'On a Saturday I usually finish at lunchtime or in the middle of the afternoon if we are busy,' she told Jonathan as they began walking back along the street. 'I like to take a picnic if the weather is nice, and I normally sit in the green for a short time before travelling home. I have been to the bakery and the fruiterer's; do you like grapes?' Jonathan simply nodded as Camille continued talking.

After nearly ten minutes walking, they finally reached a small garden with luscious green grass and flower beds that lined the dusty pathways. Bumblebees could be heard among the flowers, and the trees that surrounded them were filled with birds singing. Camille stopped at a bench and placed the basket in the middle. Jonathan took a seat.

'Do you like jam?' she asked.

'Yes.' She had bought a small crusty bread cob that had already been sliced into thick slices; there was a small pot of butter and a similar pot of jam. Using a blunt knife, she smeared the slices of bread with a generous layer of butter before returning over them with bright red strawberry jam. Jonathan's mouth was beginning to water as the warm smell of the bread and the sweet scent of the jam caused his stomach to rumble. When finished, she placed the slices back on top of the basket and gestured to Jonathan to help himself.

'This is delicious,' Jonathan said through a mouthful of bread. Camille smiled before bursting into laughter upon seeing Jonathan sheepishly trying to remove the jam that had fallen off his bread and onto his shirt.

'I have napkins.' She chuckled, reaching into the bottom of the basket. After finishing the bread between them, Camille pulled out a bunch of bright red grapes and placed them in the middle of the basket for them both the share.

'So do you intend returning to England?' she asked, breaking the moment's silence. Jonathan knew he had to be careful what he told her.

'I do intend to return home, yes, but for now I must remain in Paris.'

'Do you know for how long?' Again Jonathan paused; he had hoped to be home already.

'It could be anything up to a few months, but if it extends for too long I will move out of Monsieur and Madame Lesieur's apartment. I have taken too much of their generosity already.' Camille did not respond to this and changed the subject.

'How are you finding your work with Samuel?'

'They are friendly, and I am enjoying it.' Jonathan reached out for another grape, but squeezed one of Camille's fingers by mistake. 'I am terribly sorry,' he said, his face flushed red with embarrassment. Camille pulled back her hand but did not speak. A smile crept across her face as she looked back at him. Their eyes met, and for a split second the silence in Jonathan's mind had never sounded so loud. Camille smirked. The silence was disturbed when a dragonfly landed upon Camille's blouse, its slender body a beautiful turquoise colour, its wings gleaming in the sunlight like tiny panes of glass. It sat perfectly upon her like a brooch, and Camille gasped before realising what it was. She looked at the creature with admiration before turning her gaze back to Jonathan who was staring at the delicate animal. The moment lasted less than ten seconds, and as quickly as it had arrived, the small insect was gone.

'Let's go,' Camille finally said. She picked up the now-empty basket and led the way out of the gardens. Jonathan could not take the smile from his face.

Chapter ELEVEN

On Sunday afternoon, Camille invited Jonathan on a walk with Jack. The little terrier was a bundle of energy and marched up the street ahead of them both, clearly aware of the nearby park to which they were headed. Camille was quiet; she hadn't spoken with Jonathan much since their picnic the previous day, and had been distant with him for the majority of the morning.

'Have I done something to upset you?' Jonathan finally broke the silence as they walked through a stone arch leading into the small park.

'No, I'm sorry, it's just...' she paused. 'Yesterday during our picnic, I really enjoyed our time together. But I am afraid...'

'Afraid of me?' Jonathan was shocked.

'Afraid that if we spend too much time together, I may not wish you to leave; my grandparents take strangers in all the time, some are not so nice and take advantage of their generosity. My grandmother, Anne, gets herself far too attached to them. I know she is already attached to you, and I worry that she will be heartbroken when you leave. So many before you have left without even saying goodbye and it has always upset her so. You are a good man Jonathan; do not allow us to grow close to you if you intend to disappear like all the others.' Camille continued walking as she spoke, a slight stutter detectable as she tried to say what had clearly been a rehearsed speech; her eyes saddened by her own words. Yet despite her word of caution, Jonathan could detect that she was not thinking of herself at all, but the feelings of her beloved grandparents.

The park was quiet. As they reached the far end, Camille turned and gestured for them to turn back; Jack was in the middle of the lawn rolling in the lush green grass. Jonathan had still not spoken; he wanted to tell Camille that she was silly to worry and that everything would be okay, but in his heart he knew that going home had been the only thing keeping his spirits up over the past week. Yet despite this, he too was becoming attached to Camille and her grandparents, and knowing he would return home never to see them again was something he was already trying to push from his mind.

***

On Monday, Jonathan was met by Samuel at the front door. Samuel was his normal smiling self and spoke to Jonathan as if he were an old friend.

'We visited Sophia's parents at the weekend,' he told Jonathan, 'they live on the edge of the city.' Jonathan was amused how Samuel seemed to be able to start a conversation in a way that sounded like he was already half-way through telling it. Every time Samuel mentioned Sophia, his smile would widen. The handlebar moustache however barely moved.

Before arriving at the warehouse, Jonathan stopped off to buy a newspaper, which had become a daily ritual since he'd started his job. He was determined to keep his eye out for any mention of Madam Mystic and Le Cheval Carrousel Volant. He left the paper inside his locker for the majority of the day, bringing it out during his breaks, when he'd sit and study each and every page carefully. His French was improving, but reading it was still a little vague. Thankfully, Samuel knew without asking what he was searching for, and would read the paper in the afternoon, looking out for any mention of the carousel that Jonathan could have missed.

Every day that week he bought a newspaper, and by his second Friday he was fed up. He'd been in 1889 for nearly two weeks already, but the time seemed to have passed by in the blink of an eye. He took out his frustration on the newspaper, screwing it up and tossing it in the bin, he worried he may never get home.

Despite his enjoyment of his new found job, Jonathan was pleased that the weekend was again upon him. Before they left, Monsieur Baudin handed out the pay envelopes; this was the first time that week Jonathan had spoken to him, and a short conversation it was.

'Good work this week.'

'Thank you Monsieur Baudin.' And with that Monsieur Baudin returned to his office. Lyle ripped open his envelope straight away and inspected his money.

'Time for a drink; anybody coming?' He said, taking off his overalls and hanging them inside his locker. He was the only one who did this, the rest of them travelled home in their dirty work clothes. Lyle however would bring a spare clean shirt with him on a Friday so he looked respectable for the pub. He was much taller than Jonathan, Samuel and René, and his blonde hair and huge muscular arms certainly made him stand out.

'I'll come for a while,' René replied, washing off the oil that stained his hands and forearms.
'What about you two?' Lyle looked at Jonathan, and Jonathan looked at Samuel to see if he was planning to say yes.
'I don't see why not, just for one or two,' said Samuel, 'after all, we need to buy Jonathan a drink to welcome him into the team'. Lyle cheered at this comment and slapped Jonathan on the back. All four men left the warehouse together and within five minutes they

entered a small tavern. It was just past six o' clock and the bar was already full of people. Jonathan found himself slightly overwhelmed by it all; the room was not overly large and was filled with smoke from cigarettes and pipes and there was an overpowering smell of beer. Jonathan could barely hear Samuel as he asked him what he wanted to drink over the sound of men laughing and joking in the corners and the three bartenders shouting drinks orders back to paying customers.

'I'll have what you're having,' Jonathan shouted back to Samuel, who pushed his way through a huddle of gentlemen to reach the bar. At the end of the bar was an elderly man playing an accordion that could only just be heard above the noise. As Jonathan stood waiting for his drink, he noticed that there were no women in the bar at all, though two of the three bartenders were women. Samuel finally re-emerged from the crowd holding two pint glasses. He handed one to Jonathan and gestured towards a large support pillar in the centre of the room with a number of bar stools against it and a small ledge that would be wide enough for their pint glasses.

'How's your old lady René, when is she due?' Lyle asked as they sat in a small huddle.

'René's wife is pregnant,' Samuel lent in and whispered to Jonathan.

'The sickness is still terrible, and she is up half of the night. I will be pleased when the bloody thing arrives. She wanted four, but I can barely cope with one and it hasn't even arrived yet.' He laughed which caused his think round glasses to wobble on the bridge of his nose. 'What about you Lyle, are you still seeing that girl? What was her name, Leigh-Ann?'

'No, she went back to University in Brussels.' Lyle did not seem disappointed by this at all. In spite of only catching snippets of the conversation over the loud tavern, Jonathan was surprised to find he was enjoying himself. The pint in front of him was like nothing he had ever tasted before; it was cloudy and bitter, and left an aftertaste that started making him feel sick. Somehow though he still ended up finishing his own drink before the rest of them.

The bar seemed to get increasing busier as the night progressed, and the tables that were packed closely together slowly became invisible as they were eclipsed by the mass of people. There was a thin wooden staircase in the corner with an open landing visible to the bar below, and three closed doors that occasionally saw men enter, only to leave nearly twenty minutes later; Jonathan found himself watching the men and chuckled to himself upon finally realising what they were doing up there.

The evening quickly turned into night time, and with everybody having bought a round, Jonathan knew it was only polite to offer another drink.

'I don't know what these were; will you help me at the bar?' He asked Samuel who leaped up. The drinking did not stop there, as the four men again went around taking their turn at buying the next round, and by the end Jonathan had consumed eight full pints and was certainly more than a little tipsy.

'I think it is time I got this one back, he has been slurring his words from three pints ago,' Samuel joked, nudging Jonathan's arm. Jonathan simply laughed and got up to follow his colleagues as they left the bar.

It was dark out now and the streets were lit with bright lights coming from the bars that lined the road.

'See you on Monday then.' Lyle slapped Jonathan and the other men on the shoulder, laughing at Jonathan as he stumbled from the impact. Lyle was evidently the only one used to drinking at that kind of level, as he spoke and walked like any sober man. Lyle and René headed in the opposite direction to Jonathan and Samuel, and gave swift goodbyes. Jonathan knew he was drunk; he could feel himself swaying slightly.

'Is this something you do often with Lyle and René?' Jonathan asked.

'Every couple of weeks, but at the least at the end the month.'

The tram ride back was quicker than expected; it had very few people aboard and stopped only a handful of times. The night air felt fresh compared to the heat of the daytime. It was a clear night and under the darkened streets a few stars could be seen faintly in the sky. Samuel ensured Jonathan made it through the door of Anne and Olivier's apartment before wishing him a pleasant weekend and retreating into his own apartment. When Jonathan entered Anne and Olivier's apartment he immediately saw Olivier in his armchair in front of the small wood burner. He was fast asleep with a book balanced on his chest. A small clock sat upon the fireplace read half past twelve.

'I thought I heard you come in,' Anne whispered as she came into the room, 'have you been to the pub with Samuel?'

'Yes, I am sorry if you were expecting me at the normal time, I did not know about the pub until the end of the day.' Jonathan felt awful in case she had worried. He followed her out of the living room and towards the dining room.

'Not to worry dear, I know Samuel and the boys often go for drinks on a Friday. Let me make you a cup of tea.' She led him into the dining room away from the sleeping Olivier, and when Anne returned with the tray, Jonathan had already taken out his money envelope and had started figuring out which coins he was supposed to give her. He found the two she had told him and picked up a third one, handing all three over to her.

'Just two dear,' she said, handing one back to him with a smile.

'Are you sure that is enough though?'

'It's just perfect. Now drink up and get yourself to bed.' Jonathan did as he was told and left the table feeling a little less foggy than when he had arrived. He returned to his bedroom and was surprised to bump into Camille in the corridor. She was leaving the bathroom in her night gown and blushed upon seeing Jonathan.

'I'm sorry, I hope I did not startle you,' said Jonathan, trying his hardest not to sound drunk.

'Good night,' was all that Camille said, a smile spreading across her face as she retreated back behind her bedroom door.

Chapter TWELVE

Saturday had arrived again, and when Jonathan woke he found that Anne was the only person in the apartment. She was sat at the dining room table reading yesterday's newspaper that he'd brought back for her; Jack was fast asleep at her feet, snoring softly.

'Good morning,' said Jonathan, startling Anne and causing her to jump. Jack woke instantly to see what all the commotion was all about, and wasted no time at all pounding over to Jonathan and jumping all over him, his tail circling like a windmill.

'Let me pour you a cup of tea dear, I have only just brought through the pot.' Without even waiting for a response, she began pouring the hot tea into a clean cup.

'Has Camille gone to work?' he asked, knowing too well what the answer was.

'Yes, but she is normally home by mid-afternoon.' Jonathan wondered if it would be weird for him to take himself along to meet her; after all, he had no plans and as much as he liked Anne, he knew if he stayed she would only fuss over him the whole day.

Jonathan used the excuse that he was taking Jack for a walk. Not knowing the dog very well, he decided it was best to put him on a lead; he didn't think Camille would ever forgive him if he lost Jack.

He was impressed with himself for managing to find his way to the tram stop Camille had taken him to the week before. The carriage was busy and Jonathan spent the entire journey looking through the murky windows trying to figure out where to get off. Jack sat on his knee for the whole ride, and after ten minutes curled up on his lap to sleep.

It was nearly thirty minutes later when Jonathan finally recognised the road leading up towards the Arc de Triomphe, and emerged from the tram as quickly as possible. It didn't take long for him to find the right street, and in no time he was walking past the building where he had been fitted for his new clothes.

'Jonathan!' A voice shouted from across the street. Jonathan turned and saw Camille waving at him. She had just left a small bakery and had her little wicker basket cradled in her arm. She crossed the road and instantly knelt down to greet her beloved dog.

'What are you both doing here, are you alone?' she said, finally acknowledging Jonathan.

'I thought you may like company for your lunch, and Jack wanted to join me.'

'Oh, Jack told you this?' She smirked and tapped Jonathan on the arm. She did not say it aloud, but Jonathan could tell she was pleased to see them. Camille led the way to the small green with the huge flower displays, where Jack was let off his lead to explore whilst Jonathan and Camille sat down on the same bench as before.

'I am impressed you found your way so easily, the trams in the city can often be confusing if you do not know your way.'

'I had Jack to help me.' Camille smiled, and told Jonathan about the art gallery and how she was busy setting up for a show taking place the following weekend.

'He is a Belgian artist who is heavily influenced by the classic French styles. His use of colours is distinctive and the images feel as though they are alive. You should come to the show with me next week; most people there will be with partners.'

'Of course.' Jonathan fought to keep the grin from his face.

'How is your job at the station warehouse by the way?' Camille asked. Jonathan proceeded to tell Camille all about his experience in the pub with his colleagues, which resulted in Camille laughing so much she could barely breathe.

Once the basket was empty they returned home, yet with the weather so pleasant and the conversation so free-flowing, they were not at all in a rush.

***

The week that followed passed quickly. Jonathan continued to buy newspapers daily in the hope of seeing the carousel mentioned, and every day Samuel checked through it afterwards for him, just in case he had missed anything.

When Thursday arrived, Samuel seemed to be in a strange mood. Jonathan did not question him and waited to see if he divulged the reasons behind his distraction. He barely spoke for the entire journey to work, and when they arrived he went straight into the office to see his father. Through the large window Jonathan saw them speaking, and watched Monsieur Baudin leap to his feet and grab Samuel's hand in an exaggerated handshake. As Jonathan watched, Lyle and René arrived.

'What's going on in there?' Lyle asked, standing beside Jonathan.

'I don't know,' Jonathan admitted,' Samuel was in a strange mood this morning, but he didn't say anything.' Just then, Samuel left the office, the biggest smile across his face as he walked over to the three men.

'I suppose you vultures want to know what that was all about.' Samuel laughed, walking straight past them and opened up his locker. He pulled out his work boots and changed into them. He played on it for a few seconds longer, sniggering to himself at seeing the three men standing there impatiently. 'Well Sophia and I found out last night that we are expecting another baby.' With no hesitation the three men all rushed to shake Samuel's hand as they extended their congratulations.

'When is it due?' Asked René.

'Not until January.'

'Is it a boy or a girl?' asked Jonathan. The three men all turned and looked at him as though he was crazy.

'Well yes, it will be one of them, but I couldn't confirm which 'til the birth.' Samuel tried to sound polite, but a slight sarcasm polluted his tone. What an idiotic thing to ask, thought Jonathan. He'd momentarily forgot he was in 1889 – sexing the baby was clearly something that didn't happen here until after birth. Jonathan laughed and tried to pass off his comment as a joke, but the three men did not appear to be fooled.

Friday had finally arrived, and by the end of

Jonathan's third week he was now confident with many aspects of his work. He was often left to get on with tasks such as minor engine repairs and service jobs such as oil changes, furnace cleaning and general maintenance of the trams and locomotives. The Friday newspaper again had nothing about the carousel or Madam Mystic, and after three weeks of trying, Jonathan was beginning to wonder if he was wasting his time.

As the day came to a close, Monsieur Baudin came out of the office and handed out the envelopes containing their week's wage. It amused Jonathan that this was the only time he ever saw Monsieur Baudin out of the office, and still he barely spoke unless absolutely necessary.

'Drink tonight fellas, to celebrate our Samuel becoming a father for the second time.' Lyle was always the most eager to visit the pub on Fridays, and would find any kind of reason as to why they should all have a drink.

'I can't this week,' said Jonathan before the other two could agree, 'Camille has some art show on tonight and she asked me to go with her.'

'Oh?' Lyle stopped what he was doing and turned to face Jonathan, 'is this a date?'

'I don't know, she asked me so she wouldn't be the only one there without a date, so maybe.'

'Leave the man alone Lyle,' Samuel cut in, 'I too will have to pass on drinks tonight, but next Friday will be fine.'

René agreed to join Lyle at the pub, and upon leaving Lyle shouted back: 'we will make sure to have one for you Samuel, a toast to the baby.'

The journey home was a complete contrast to that of the morning commute; Samuel could not stop talking about Sophia and the new baby and how excited they both were to be extending their family. 'Frédéric will enjoy being a big brother, and the new baby will arrive in January about one month before Frédéric's birthday,' he told Jonathan, his words coming out faster and faster.

When Jonathan returned to the apartment, Camille was already home and standing in the sitting room. She was wearing a large evening dress, an elegant gown of sky blue damask with a pattern of pink chrysanthemum petals and layers of embroidered lace tulle; she wore long white gloves up to her elbows with a fan clutched in her right hand. Her hair was pinned up with a feathered headdress. Finally, around her neck she wore a pearl choker which sat perfectly. Jonathan was speechless. Camille smiled shyly before speaking.

'You only need to change into your smart shoes, a fresh shirt and the black jacket you got from the tailor. I asked Papi if you could borrow one of his ties, oh, and a hat, most gentlemen will be wearing one. I left everything in your room upon your bed so you did not have to worry what to wear.' Jonathan did not reply, and simply edged passed Camille, his eyes fixated upon her the entire time.

It didn't take long for Jonathan to change; he wore the smart shoes that he had arrived in Paris wearing, and his new smart clothes were getting their first wear. The jacket also came with a matching waistcoat, but he wasn't sure whether he should wear it this evening. With the image of the dress Camille was wearing still stuck firmly in his mind, Jonathan decided that he should. A top hat had been left on his bed along with a cravat. He placed the hat upon his head and dashed back out to the sitting room where Camille was more than happy to assist with the cravat.

There was a knock on the door. Anne came into the sitting room and gushed over them both as she went to answer. 'You both look incredible.' She opened the door and found Samuel standing in the stairwell. 'Come in, come in.' Anne said, her voice echoing up into the vestibule.

'I cannot, I just wish to speak with Jonathan quickly before he leaves for the evening.' Jonathan heard this and headed straight for the door, joining Samuel in the stairwell and closing the door behind him. Samuel had a serious look upon his face that worried Jonathan slightly.

'I am sorry to disturb you when you are going out for the evening,' said Samuel politely, 'but what I need to tell you could not wait.'

'What is it?'

'Sophia took Frédéric down to the Exposition today; whilst she was there, she told me that Frédéric rode on a carousel that had only just been set up by the river below the Eiffel tower. She could not remember the name of the carousel, but she did say a fortune teller was positioned next to it. I can't be certain, but it could be Madam Mystic and Le Cheval Carrousel Volant. You need to go check it out, as it may not stay past the weekend.' Jonathan thanked Samuel, who immediately headed back into his own apartment. His mind began to race as he stood there in between the two apartment doors. How he wanted to race down to the Eiffel tower and find this carousel! How he wanted it to be the one that could take him home. But what about Camille? He had promised to be her date for the evening, he couldn't just run out on her.

Chapter THIRTEEN

Camille had a horse and carriage waiting outside to take them to the gallery – it had been arranged by her employer Madame Caballé. A young boy sat on top of the closed-top carriage, grasping a pair of thick black leather reins that he used to steer the two black and white horses that stood waiting. Within seconds of entering the carriage, the young boy shouted 'away now,' and they took off down the street.

Jonathan could not take his eyes off Camille for the whole journey. Her dazzling caramel skin and dark brown hair caught the sparkle of her headpiece, making her appear even more radiant and sophisticated. Her long gown trailed slightly against the floor and was fit for a princess. They barely spoke at all during the journey, but instead looked out at the evening sky that was already turning dark. The moon was already visible in the sky, and hung bright and full above the bustling city. Camille watched out of the window as traffic raced by in all directions. Her hair blew gently in the breeze, and yet Jonathan could not wrench his thoughts from the carousel Samuel had told him about near the tower. Could it really be the one?

The carriage took them around the Arc de Triomphe, and from Jonathan's window he saw the Eiffel Tower lit up above the buildings. When Jonathan and Camille arrived at the gallery, it was shortly after seven o' clock. The art show was not supposed to start for another thirty minutes but Camille was expected to help fill champagne glasses ready for the arrival of guests. The gallery director Madame Caballé was already slightly tipsy. She was a large woman with a crooked smile and black hair that sat upon her head in one big heap, a thin silver pin holding it all in one place. She had huge pendants on chains around her neck that sparkled off the gallery spotlights, and her fingers were lined with elaborate jewellery. Her makeup was subtle, yet her outfit was bold and colourful with heavy patterns that started at her high neck line and extended down to the floor. She was the kind of woman who seemed to find everything funny, and laughed after everything she said, a high pitched chortle that caused her entire body to shake. She had a habit of cutting into other people's sentences with her own thoughts if she found their speech to be of little interest.

'Now Camille, once our guests arrive you are to circulate among them. Make sure everybody knows who you are,' she said with yet another chuckle, 'and remember we want to sell as many paintings tonight as possible, so carry a handful of sold labels with you just in case.' She again laughed, this time snorting accidently, which only caused her to laugh even more.

A tall man entered the gallery, and Madame Caballé threw herself towards the doorway to greet him, gesturing back for Camille to hand him a glass of champagne.

'Monsieur Degas, please allow me to show you how I have arranged your painting, follow me.' Madame Caballé led the gentleman around the large open gallery, stopping before each painting in turn before leading him into a second room where more paintings were displayed. Camille leaned in and confirmed what Jonathan was already suspecting.

'That is the artist – he is the best we have ever hosted, and it is a real honour to have him choose us for his show.' Within minutes of Madame Caballé leading the French artist into the second room, a flurry of people began to descend from the street. Camille and Jonathan frantically handed out the champagne flutes, and within thirty minutes the gallery was bursting with life, and people outside still queuing to get inside. Camille had been dragged away by Madame Caballé to meet the artist as well as other art lovers, artists and gallery owners. Jonathan was left filling glasses of champagne alone as more people continued to filter through the door; it was nearly an hour before the arrivals ceased. With Camille distracted, Jonathan was contemplating leaving and heading down to the Exposition area in the hope of finding the carousel; he knew that if it wasn't the right one he could easily be back in time before Camille had even noticed him gone. But what if it was the right one? What if he left the gallery now and never saw Camille again? He would feel awful having not said goodbye. He decided that seeing Camille first was the right thing to do – he would tell her he was going to take a short walk to get some fresh air, which was not unbelievable with the gallery so busy. He had seen Camille be led through into the second gallery room, and he began squeezing his way through the masses of people towards the door. It was only now that he began to take notice of the artwork they had all crowded in to see. The first gallery room was filled with paintings featuring ballet dancers, all of which showcased young girls in long ballet gowns during rehearsals in a dance studio. The paintings were getting a lot of attention, and many already had 'sold' labels pinned to them. As Jonathan entered the next gallery room, he was instantly faced with *Woman Combing Her Hair*, a painting portraying a naked woman holding up her hair as she combs the underside, her buttocks cheekily on display at the base of the painting, her arm raised holding her hair, a slight glimpse of her left breast just visible. As Jonathan made his way further into the room, he noticed that the painting was one of many in a series; the same woman could be seen numerous times around the room. She was undressing for a bath in one, crouching inside a metal tub in another, and then drying herself off. Again Jonathan noticed that many of these too were labelled as sold.

'Camille,' Jonathan finally reached her through the crowd; her face was flushed due to the overwhelming heat in the gallery.

'I am popping outside for some air; I may take a walk to stretch my legs. I will be back shortly.'

'Okay,' said Camille, unable to say anything more as Madame Caballé dragged her off to be introduced to yet another gentleman.

Jonathan took off the top hat he had been wearing and wiped his forehead that was sodden with sweat. Without a moment to lose, Jonathan took off back towards the Arc de Triomphe where he knew he'd be able to see the top of the tower above the buildings. Upon reaching the Arc he stopped to catch his breath. The tower now glowed in the night sky and Jonathan again sped in its direction as quickly as he could.

Over twenty minutes after leaving the gallery, Jonathan reached the riverside. He could see the Eiffel tower at the opposite side was lit up by hundreds of gas lamps, while a beacon at the very top sent out three beams of red, white and blue light. His mind firmly on the carousel, Jonathan first checked the treeline where he had originally been dropped by it, but the area was empty. He then crossed the river and navigated his way under the tower to the small green with the large water fountains, but again a carousel was nowhere to be seen. Jonathan was on the verge of giving up; he had no idea where exactly it was supposed to be, and it may have already packed up and left. Disheartened, he made his way back under the tower and along the bridge, stopping half way to catch his breath once more. Looking out over the darkened water, he saw below him a walkway that led along the edge of the river and under the bridge he stood upon. Peeking out from the shadows, Jonathan saw a carousel. His heart skipped a beat as he took off back along the bridge where he located a narrow set of stone steps leading down to the passageway below.

As he reached the edge of the shadows, the carousel became clearer to him. It was certainly of a similar design, but he could tell straight away that it was not Le Cheval Carrousel Volant. Exhausted and deflated, Jonathan sat on the edge of the carousel; his legs drained of energy from all the running.

'I am never going to get home,' he said to himself, throwing his face into his hands and letting out a loud sigh.

'Now then young man,' came the unexpected voice of a woman, 'what brings you to the underpass?' A haggard old beggar woman emerged from the shadows. She pulled behind her a cart filled with what Jonathan suspected were her belongings. Jonathan stood as she came closer to him, feeling overdressed in her company. Her hair was windswept and her tattered clothes were worn and dirty. Jonathan wrinkled his nose.

'I'm sorry, I did not mean to disturb you,' said Jonathan, turning to leave, but as he did so she grabbed his arm using the handle of her umbrella and pulled him back.

'Young men like you should be careful, a big city like this is not always safe.'

'Would you too not be better off somewhere safer than the shadows?' Jonathan asked. She hesitated, clearly not expecting Jonathan's reply.

'The shadows are where I am at my best. In the shadows you can observe the passers-by more clearly, and with better chance of going unnoticed.'

'I'm sorry to say that I have nothing of value with me.' He placed his hands inside his trouser pockets to check.

'You have something much more valuable than money young man,' the woman's voice croaked, 'you have knowledge, you have knowledge of things to come, and you have a secret that you dare not share.' She smiled as she said this.

Jonathan looked hard at her. 'Who are you?' he demanded.

'Oh just a simple beggar woman. I tell fortunes to earn money in the day. Some people are difficult to read, and so I make it up, but you are the easiest face to read I have ever met. When I look at you I can see everything in your eyes, you're an open person and a good man. I can also see you are not from here – you stand out so such, and you seek a way home.'

'How do you know all this?'

'It is a gift, young man.'

'So answer me this: will I get home?'

'There will be an opportunity. By the fourth new moon, what you need to go home will be there; but by then what you have here will not be so easy to give up.'

'What do you mean?' His voice a stutter. Slowly the woman turned and edged her way back into the shadows. 'Wait, come back.' He called after her, but she disappeared into the darkness. A chill shot up Jonathan's spin. He did not wait around and made his way back to the gallery as quickly as he could.

The walk seemed to take much longer this time; Jonathan dragged his feet slightly as he made his way through the city, the words of the old woman ringing in his ears. Could she really have known his secret, or was she simply talking in rhymes?

Eventually, Jonathan arrived back outside the gallery. The large windows beamed light out into the darkened street. Inside, Jonathan could see many people still socialising. Above the window was the gallery's sign: 'Madame Caballé Presents: Galarie 24.' Below the official sign was a temporary banner advertising the evening's show, simply reading: 'Vitrine d'art de M. Edgar Degas – Vendredi 21 Juin 1889,' which loosely translated to: 'Art Showcase by Mister Edgar Degas, Friday June 21st 1889.' Jonathan stared at the date for the longest of times. Tomorrow would mark three weeks since he'd arrived in Paris, but somehow it felt as though he had been here forever.

Chapter FOURTEEN

The remainder of June passed by in the blink of an eye. As the height of summer approached, so too did temperatures begin to soar. When July arrived, Jonathan found himself feeling homesick. The thoughts of his worried parents kept him awake at night, and despite his bride-to-be Nicola standing him up, he still desired to see her, even if only to ask her why she'd deserted him.

Working at the station warehouse with Samuel kept Jonathan's mind occupied for a portion of the day, and his new friends and colleagues always seemed to brighten his mood. Most Fridays he and Samuel would join Lyle and René at the pub for an after-work drink, and more often than not it would turn into a late night that often saw Jonathan a little worse for wear. Despite there still being no news of the carousel, Jonathan continued to buy the newspaper on a daily basis in the hope of finding any mention of Le Cheval Carrousel Volant. Samuel never once looked as though he begrudged helping Jonathan scan the papers.

By the end of July, Jonathan had been working at the warehouse for eight weeks. He was impressed with the amount he had learnt in such a short time, and was now regularly working alone on tasks. He was now even driving the trams back and forth between the warehouse and the transport depot, a job he enjoyed as it meant getting out of the stuffy warehouse for an hour or two.

Jonathan loved his new job, but like most people he lived for the weekends. Every Saturday he would wake and spend the morning with Anne, who would force feed him breakfast and supply him with endless amounts of hot tea. Afterwards he would take Jack for a walk, which always resulted in them meeting Camille after work and joining her for a picnic lunch. Each week Camille would purchase snacks for them to eat, and despite Jonathan offering her money for the goods, she always refused. With his wage at the end of July being his eighth consecutive payment, Jonathan had now saved up a sizeable amount of money; after paying his rent to Anne and taking out his tram fares and Friday drinking money, he very rarely spent the rest, and decided that with this money he would like to take Camille out for dinner somewhere upmarket. As they sat in their usual spot in the park watching Jack rolling in the grass, Jonathan finally perked up the courage to ask her.

'I was wondering if I could take you out for dinner one evening as a thank you for these delicious lunch hampers you allow me to share with you each week.'

'Where were you thinking of taking me?' she asked whilst tucking into the final few berries she had in the wicker basket.

'Oh. Erm.' Jonathan hadn't actually thought of a particular restaurant. 'Where would you like to go?'

'Well, there is a restaurant I have wanted to go

to for a while now, but it is not cheap.'

'Price is not a concern; I have been saving up my wage for some time now. Tell me about this restaurant.'

'It is called Le Grand Colbert, it would be a carriage ride away from home, but they are known for doing some of the best seafood dishes in city. Do you like seafood?' she asked, noticing Jonathan's expression turn somewhat.

'Yes, I just wasn't expecting to hear seafood as your first choice of restaurant.' Jonathan smirked. He himself had had very little experience with seafood, mostly due to his own lack of interest. Yet still he agreed to the restaurant and promised he would make all the arrangements.

Over the course of the following week, with the help of Samuel, Jonathan found the details for the restaurant and made reservations for his dinner date with Camille. He booked a table for seven o'clock on Friday evening, and arranged for a carriage to collect them as well as take them home afterwards. Camille was so excited that she spent the entire week talking about it; she even took a long lunch break on the

Wednesday before in order to buy a new dress.

'It is dark blue,' she told Anne over dinner that night, 'and has a beautiful embroidered pattern of birds and golden leaves. It has a bateau neckline, and the short sleeves have lace at the end.'

'It sounds wonderful dear,' replied Anne.

'Oh and Mémé, I have not told you about the wonderful hat that goes with it. It is again dark blue, and it has blue roses on top which each have sequins on to make them sparkle in the light.' Jonathan could not help but sit and smile as he watched Camille get herself even more excited. He tried to picture what she was describing but he had never been very good when it came to using his imagination. Thankfully he did not have to wait long, and when Friday arrived and he got home from work, Camille was already wearing her new dress and hat.

'You look beautiful,' He said, kissing her hand that again wore white gloves. She blushed and told him to hurry into his clean clothing, as the carriage would be arriving to collect them at any moment.

It took over half an hour to reach the

restaurant by carriage. It was at a part of the city Jonathan was not so familiar with, and was situated on a tiny narrow street that could only accommodate their carriage. The exterior of the restaurant was slender, yet its wood-framed windows dominating the exterior, a complete contrast to the rest of the stone building that ran the entire length of the street. Camille did not wait for Jonathan to open the door for her, and marched ahead of him and through the doorway.

Stepping inside the restaurant was like stepping through a portal. The small but lovely exterior belied the 100-seat brasserie that plunged deep into the building. The Belle Époque style interior was divided into three sections by etched glass screens. The mosaic flooring was an instant eye-catcher that started in the doorway and led along the extensive bar and throughout the restaurant, and ceiling mouldings high above gave the restaurant a certain grandeur. The bar with its painted friezes ran down one side of the room, and giant ferns sprouted everywhere, giving the place a softer touch. Rich velvet curtains draped along walls and around the edges of the windows, and copper globe lamps glimmered against the multitude of mirrors that lined the walls, handfuls of which were covered in theatre posters. Long black leather banquettes formed most of the seating around the edges of the room, and the remaining tables had strong wooden chairs with simple padded seats. All the tables were laid with the whitest table clothes, and the polished silver cutlery shone against the candles upon each table.

The restaurant was already busy, and within seconds of entering Jonathan and Camille were directed to a table in the corner. The waiter was tall and lean, and wore a handlebar moustache similar to Samuel's.

'May I offer you a drink Madam?' He took out a notebook and pencil from the pocket of his apron and waited patiently for her reply.

'A glass of white wine please,' said Camille, glancing over a drinks menu quickly in case something else caught her eye; she then looked at Jonathan, eager to hear what he would order.

'Make that a bottle,' Jonathan spoke to the waiter before turning his gaze back on Camille. 'I will join you with some wine,' he said. Camille smiled at him. Jonathan turned to the menu. After spending two months reading newspapers, his French reading was now a lot better. Moments later the waiter returned to take their order. 'Would you like starters?' he asked, holding out his notepad ready.

'Yes, I would like the whelks please, and for main I will try the herring.' Camille put down her menu and gave Jonathan an excitable smile. Jonathan was trying to figure out what a whelk was and momentarily forgot what he had intended to order.

'And for you, Sir?' The waiter was becoming impatient.

'Oh, yes.' Jonathan glanced back at his menu to remind himself. 'I think I will take the soup to start, and the roasted chicken for main.'

'Very good Sir, can I offer you an aperitif?'

'Could we get a Lillet blanc each?' Camille spoke for them both. The waiter nodded, tucked his notepad back into his pocket and took away their menus.

While they waited for their food, Jonathan could not stop wondering what it was Camille had ordered, but he refrained from asking in case it was something obvious that would only make him sound silly. As he was presented with a large oval-shaped bowl of vegetable soup, Camille was given a plate of sea snails. The smell was overpowering. Jonathan politely declined when she offered him one to try.

'Would you care to try one?' Camille gestured towards her plate. Jonathan's eye widened, his nostrils flared as he took in the smell coming from her plate.

'I think I will pass this time.' He said tucking into his hot soup. Camille smiled and proceeded to eat her snails; they were presented in an oval dish, with a garlic sauce. She used a small folk in which to extract the meat from the shell, and Jonathan could not stop watching her as she did this.

'What do they taste like?' He asked once she had finally finished.

'Have you never tried them? She seemed genuinely shocked. 'They only really taste of the sauce they are cooked in, with a texture similar to a mushroom. I will have to get Mémé Anne to make you a bowl, she is a talent with snails and seafood.' Jonathan stayed quiet, he wished he had never asked.

The main course was not far behind and again Jonathan was curious to know what Camille's dish would be like. He had a sizzling half-chicken with vegetables and potatoes, the smell of which rushed into his nostrils as the plate was laid before him, his mouth instantly watering. However, the smell of his dinner was soon drowned out by Camille's, as a full herring fish, still with scales and eyes, was laid before her. Her eyes lit up at the sight of it, but Jonathan could not think of anything worse.

'Have you always been a fan of seafood?' He asked, watching her devour the fish.

'Oh yes,' she replied, 'my father was a fisherman in the town of Tréhiguier from an early age. My mother was a great lover of seafood and so I was raised on so many varieties of fish.' Her eyes lit as she spoke about her parents, yet behind the smile a sense of sadness was evident.

'You must really miss them.'

'I do,' she sighed, 'I think of them every day.'

'How old were you when they died?' Jonathan was cautious not to come across noisy.

'I was seven. We had come to Paris to visit

my grandparents and on the second night my parents went out for dinner alone. They never made it to the restaurant. The carriage they took capsized as the horses lost control; unfortunately the carriage tipped over in front of a moving tram. The young horse handler lost his life that night too.' Jonathan passed Camille his handkerchief as tears cascaded down her face.

'I'm sorry, I did not mean to make you cry.'

'No, I am sorry, we were supposed to be enjoying ourselves and I have ruined the evening,'

'You could never ruin anything. I know how much it means to open up about things and tell somebody what you are going through. I'm just pleased you know you can talk to me.' Camille smiled at his comment and wiped away her tears. She sat up straight in her chair and looked to change the subject. They talked about Anne and Olivier, as well as Samuel and his wife Sophia. There was even a brief discussion about going for dinner again sometime.

After a small dessert and a coffee, Jonathan was slightly disappointed to find it was time to leave. They had talked non-stop since being seated, and it had been nice to break up their normal routine of eating in the apartment with Anne and Olivier. Jonathan paid the bill at the bar, away from Camille so she did not know the full cost. It was certainly expensive, but thankfully he had enough.

Less than five minutes later they were back in the carriage making their way home. It was getting late and the city streets were finally slowing down for the night, and with their moods so uplifted the sound of the horses' hooves against the cobbled roads felt almost tuneful as they made their way through Paris.

'Thank you for dinner Jonathan. It was a most pleasant evening.' She lent in and kissed him on the cheek. Even in the darkness of the cab she could see that his face had turned red. Wishing to return the gesture, but knowing that 1889 was probably not the era to suddenly snog her, Jonathan found some romance within him, and did something that surprised even himself. Jonathan gently took hold of Camille's hand, and very carefully removed the white glove to expose her nimble fingers; he then gently raised her hand to his lips and kissed it. Camille let out a small giggle before retreating her hand, and the pair of them sat arm in arm listening to the city noises without muttering another word all the way back.

Chapter FIFTEEN

As the weeks past, even Samuel could see Jonathan was becoming more and more disgruntled at the fact he was still no closer to finding Madam Mystic or the carousel. One particular Friday at the end of August saw the hottest day of the summer. Hot, bothered and frustrated, Jonathan screwed up the newspaper and threw it into the bin without even asking Samuel to look through it as he normally would. The frustration was getting to him, and he was now struggling to keep it to himself. Despite his dismay, his work never once suffered, and although small signs were being detected back at home, he managed to keep an optimistic attitude around Anne, Olivier and Camille.

Every Saturday in August without fail, Jonathan would travel through to the city centre and search the areas around the Eiffel tower before abandoning his hunt and meeting Camille for lunch in their usual spot. Finally, September brought its cooling breeze and a fresh feel to the city and its residents. By now, Jonathan was slowing beginning to give up hope of ever returning home, and on Wednesday the twenty-fifth of September, for the first time since arriving in Paris, he did not buy a newspaper at all. Samuel noticed this and offered to purchase one during their lunch break, but Jonathan simply refused. He had now been in Paris for over seventeen weeks, and although in the grand scheme of things he was having an enjoyable experience, the past few weeks had seen him homesick.

Friday arrived yet again, and in a bid to cheer Jonathan up, Samuel, Lyle and René took him to the pub. It had been a few weeks since they had all been out and they hoped some light-hearted conversation and a few beers would put a smile on his face.

The pub, as always, was packed, but they

managed to grab the last free table. The accordion player who seemed to be in most nights was again in the corner trying to be heard above the noise of the crowd. Being with his work friends was always an enjoyable time for Jonathan; the three of them could not have been any more different from one another, and yet they all got on so well. Samuel, who was expecting his second child, was more interested in talking about that, while René, who was about to become a father for the first time any day now, happily dropped in and out of discussions with him. Lyle, who was single, found it boring and would always try to encourage Jonathan into conversations about women. He was particularly interested to know more about him and Camille.

'Are you still meeting her each Saturday for lunch?' he asked.

'Yes,' shouted Jonathan over the noise of the bar. 'Why do you ask?'

'Has she still not kissed you since that night you took her out all those weeks ago? Sounds to me like she isn't interested, you must be a terrible kisser.' Lyle snorted a laugh. Jonathan had told them all about the night at the restaurant, but he had refrained from speaking about Camille since. It was true they had not kissed since, but flirting had certainly been apparent between them both. Outside of the apartment Camille would hold his hand and flirt unashamedly, but in front of Anne and Olivier she'd back off. Jonathan wasn't sure why she felt the need to keep this from them, but for the time being he was happy to go along with it. Samuel already knew all this, as Jonathan had confided in him on their tram journeys to and from work, and Jonathan's opinions of Lyle's mockery must have shown in his displeased face, as Samuel butted in.

'And how is your love life going, Lyle? Samuel gave a smirk, and Lyle changed the subject.

'Let's get another drink in,' Lyle stood and downed the remaining dregs of his pint before skulking off to the bar. He returned, not with four pints for beer, but instead with four glasses of whisky. 'Get these down you ladies.' He mocked, pushing them along the table. Surprisingly it was René who picked up his glass first, holding it up to gesture 'Cheers' before downing it in one gulp. The three remaining men burst into a fit of laughter.

'It's always the quiet ones.' Jonathan sniggered.

On the journey home from the bar, Samuel also invited Jonathan and Camille around for tea on Saturday afternoon with his family. It came as quite a surprise at first, as apart from the Friday evening pub sessions, Jonathan had never spent any time with Samuel out of work.

When Jonathan told Camille about the invitation to tea she seemed overjoyed; it was very rare they got out of the apartment on a social call, so even just going across the landing seemed more exciting to her than staying home.

***

Saturday afternoon arrived in a heartbeat, and Camille put on one of her best day dresses for the occasion. Jonathan felt an edge of nerves; he had not really spoken with Samuel's wife Sophia, and he hoped the conversation would be easy. Jonathan knocked on the apartment door, and within seconds

Samuel answered with his usual smile across his face. 'Come in, come in.' He stood back and guided them into his small sitting room before closing the door behind them. Camille handed over a small cake, baked by Anne that very morning.

'Just a small gesture,' she said, handing it to Samuel, 'my grandmother makes the best orange sponge.'

'Thank you, Sophia loves Anne's orange cake; she will be thrilled to see this. Please follow me through to the dining room.' The apartment was laid out almost as a mirror image to Anne and Olivier's, but the furniture was much bolder in colour. On the way to the dining room, a painting on the wall caught the eye of Camille.

'Is this you Samuel?' she asked. Samuel turned and immediately looked embarrassed. The painting on the wall showed a man in bed, he was completely nude, with white sheets covering the majority of his body, including his more delicate parts; but it was the handlebar moustache and cheesy grin that confirmed it was most certainly Samuel.

'It is, yes.'

'This is a good piece, who is the artist?' Camille asked, looking deeper into the eyes of the painted Samuel.

'That would be me.' A voice came through from the other room; it was Samuel's wife Sophia. 'I painted that a week after our wedding whilst we were on honeymoon. Samuel of course hates that I have it on display, but I think it is the best one I have ever painted.'

'I did not know you were an artist. Are you still painting?' Before she replied, Sophia gestured for them to continue into the dining room where she had laid out a lavish afternoon tea for them. Sandwiches and pastries lined the table, and Sophia was overcome with joy upon seeing the orange cake.

'Please take a seat and I will pour the tea.' In the light of the dining room, the pregnant Sophia's baby bump became more noticeable. She was nearly six months pregnant yet she looked as though she was already fit to burst.

'I always forget you work at the art gallery Camille, how long have you been there now?'

'A little over a year; have you ever shown your

art in a show?'

'My art was something I was never confident with; I taught it for some years before meeting Samuel, but I never saw myself as an artist. I hope one day to return to the classroom and teach again.' Sophia handed out the China tea cups, the smell of fresh tea filling the air. Samuel cut up the cake, and the tea was joined by the scent of sweet orange sponge. Jonathan's felt his mouth begin to water.

The afternoon turned into Camille and Sophia talking non-stop about art. Jonathan and Samuel did not mind; they enjoyed seeing them getting along so well.

'Have you thought of any baby names yet for the new arrival?' Camille unexpectedly changed the subject. Sophia's eyes lit up and she put down her cup.

'If it is a girl we were thinking of Inès,' said Sophia, looking at her husband and smiling warmly at him, 'but we are yet to decide on a boy's name.'

'What a beautiful name, I once knew a girl called Inès,' Camille replied.

'It will be you next my dear,' Sophie looked at

both Camille and Jonathan. Samuel choked on his tea, coughing and spluttering.

'No dear,' he managed, quickly interrupted his wife and seeing the embarrassment on both Camille and Jonathan's faces, 'they are not a couple, simply good friends whilst Jonathan is in the city.'

'Oh I do beg your pardon.' Sophia looked horrified and began clearing away the tea cups at once. All of a sudden Camille burst into laughter, which caused Sophia to stop what she was doing and join in with her; within seconds all four of them were howling.

'Before you go,' said Sophia as she and Samuel walked them back to the doorway, 'I was wondering if you both would like to join us for an evening out in a couple of weeks – I believe it is Sunday the sixth of October, but I will check and let you know.'

'Is there a special occasion?' asked Camille, glancing at Jonathan.

'My father is an events manager who works with new venues on their launches. He has been working for months with the owner and manager of this new place and tells me it is like nothing Paris has ever seen before; he has given me four tickets to the opening night, it's a dinner and theatre evening in the Pigalle district.'

'What do you say?' Camille turned to Jonathan.

'Yes, well, if it is something you would like to do, let's go.' Jonathan didn't really understand what he had agreed to, but an evening out seemed like fun.

'Spectacular,' Sophia said whilst kissing Camille on the cheek goodbye, 'my father has arranged for a carriage to collect us at eight o'clock, and it will bring us back afterwards.'

Camille practically skipped across the hallway. 'I will need a new dress, I have never been to a dinner theatre show before, I wonder what it will be like.' Jonathan laughed at her giddiness, yet in the back of his mind he was shocked to hear that October was already creeping up on them. Sophia's comment about him and Camille being a couple also preyed on his mind that evening, and he couldn't shake the words from his head all night. It also made him realise that it had been weeks since he had thought of his family back home, and the guilt played on his mind causing him a restless night's sleep.

Chapter SIXTEEN

Camille spent a large amount of the day getting ready for their evening out. Even Anne was excited about them attending a new music hall opening, and helped Camille with her hair and makeup. Olivier spent most of the day as he did every Sunday afternoon, hidden behind yesterday's newspaper asleep. Anne had spent the past few weeks surrounded by fabric as she went about making a new dress for Camille. Despite living with them for so long, Jonathan was still amazed by Anne's rich past – she'd been a dress maker in her youth and had worked with some of the most lavish fabrics and artistic designers in Paris. Now retired, she still enjoyed making her granddaughter the occasional dress, and the opening of a new theatre gave her the perfect excuse.

'I worked for Charles Frederick Worth for over thirty years,' she told Jonathan whilst putting the finishing touches on the dress, 'he is an Englishman just like you. A charming man who makes the best dresses in Paris. When Charles first started, he hired only a handful of dress makers, myself included, and over time the reputation of our work grew and we were soon requested to make gowns for royalty. I was there nearly thirty years, and retired only last year. His company has grown so large – from a handful of employees to now over one thousand people.' Anne's face glowed as she spoke about her past employer – she was clearly very proud of her career and even now, as she made her granddaughter a dress, she was certain to maintain the highest of standards.

When Camille finally emerged, Jonathan was speechless, more so for the fact that Anne had created this stunning dress simply from a pile of fabric. The dress was a deep red that tucked in beautifully at Camille's waist before falling to the floor. With a black satin panel up the front and long sleeves to help keep out the chill of the night air, it was a dress worthy of the Queen. Her hair was pinned up in a bun high on the back of the head, with curls dangling around her ears on the side. As always, her hands were covered in the most delicate of lace gloves – this time they were black, which gave the whole outfit a gothic feel to it. Jonathan too had a new outfit for the occasion, and for the first time in his life he wore a fully tailored black tie suit with a crisp white shirt and bowtie; a top hat upon his head finished off the outfit. He normally hated wearing suits, and hats had never been his thing, yet the customs of late 1880 Paris did not seem to faze him one bit.

The carriage arrived at eight o'clock as expected, and Jonathan and Camille met Samuel and Sophia in the stairwell. Samuel too was wearing a tuxedo, which amused Jonathan as he was so used to seeing him in his work overalls; the black tie however suited him, and he had even put extra wax on his handlebar moustache for the evening. Sophia looked radiant in an all-black dress, the fabric framing her pregnant belly.

The carriage took them through the darkened

streets of Paris – it being a Sunday, the streets were much quieter than normal.

'I am told that this new music hall is where the White Queen Dance Hall used to stand. My father tells me it is unrecognisable now – the new owners redesigned the building inside and out.' Sophia seemed just as excited to be attending this evening's event as Camille was.

'Is it still being called the White Queen?' Camille asked.

'No, I've forgotten its new name; it has been in the paper a lot these past few weeks, but it has slipped my mind.' As the carriage turned onto Boulevard de Clichy, the scene from the cab window suddenly changed and the road was flocked with hundreds of people. Horses and carts tried to drop off their passengers as close to the venue as possible, but struggled to pass through the sea of people. It appeared as though the whole of Paris had turned up for the opening. Finally, their own carriage came to a stop, and the driver opened up the door for them to exit. They were instantly mesmerised by the spectacular building that stood before them. Lit up bright against the backdrop of a darkened street, the music hall demanded to be seen - the lower half of the building was white-washed, but above the modest entrance, standing tall above the street, was a bright red and slowly rotating windmill that lit up the night sky. In front of the windmill were large free-standing letters that read 'Moulin Rouge.'

The four of them stood silent for a moment, taking in the atmosphere and the shimmering structure that had the entire street in awe.

'I have always wanted to visit Moulin Rouge.' Jonathan spoke without thinking.

'Pardon?' Camille looked at him, her eyebrows raised.

'Oh, I mean…I meant I have always wanted to visit a Parisian music hall.' Camille smiled and took hold of his hand as they crossed the road and headed for the door. The crowds were thick and navigating their way through was no easy feat – queues of people stood waiting to get in, but three security men at the door were so far only allowing entrance to those on the guest list. One of the men took their names, and ushered them through the open doorway into a lavish corridor with a bright red carpet and wallpaper to match. Within seconds, a middle-aged gentleman came racing towards them with his arms thrust in the air.

'My darling, you are here!' It was Sophia's father, and he swooped her up into a bear hug. 'I am pleased you and your friends are here at last. Come, I want to introduce you to the owner.' He took Sophia by the arm and led her through the grand corridor where, standing next to the doorway that led into the auditorium, were two gentlemen. 'My dear daughter, I would like to introduce you to Monsieur Joseph Oller, the owner of Le Moulin Rouge, and Monsieur Charles Zidler, who is the manager.' Sophia shook the gentlemen's hands and turned to introduce Samuel, as well as Jonathan and Camille.

'A pleasure to meet you all,' Monsieur Oller said with a huge smile across his face as he shook each of them by the hand, 'I do hope you enjoy your evening, and be sure to tell your friends about it.' His large white beard twitched and his rosy cheeks glowed. The four of them were then moved along as the number of people trying to get through to the auditorium was growing fast.

The theatre hall was enormous and was split into many levels so that each table was slightly higher than the one in front, meaning everybody had a clear view. There was also a mezzanine level upstairs with a similar layout. A vast dancefloor dominated the downstairs area and a large orchestra situated on a raised stage was already playing upbeat tunes, adding to the excitable mood. The whole place was extravagantly decorated with exotic golds and reds. The immense dance hall was surrounded with seating galleries and many people had already taken their seats, ready for the entertainment to begin.

There was an air of nerves and expectation in the room as the orchestra silenced and Monsieur Zidler took to the centre of the dancefloor. 'Mesdames et Messieurs, I am honoured to welcome you tonight to La Moulin Rouge. Together we will make history this evening as you witness the birth of Paris' newest theatre, which I hope will soon become a temple of music and dance for all Parisians to enjoy.' The hundreds of people crammed into the hall clapped, and soon the orchestra began to play once more, providing the fanfare for a swarm of female dancers who came out to grace the dancefloor.

Champagne flowed the entire night, and after each performance came a minute's break before the next big number began. The dancers were mostly women, but the occasional male dancer would appear in certain routines. The elaborate cabaret-style costumes seemed to get bigger and bolder as the night progressed, and the audience clapped and cheered after each act. As the evening developed, the dance routines and costumes began to become more and more daring, with lower-cut necklines and dresses that showed more than just the ankles.

All at once the room fell into silence and the lighting dimmed. A line of women walked to the centre of the dancefloor and, as the orchestra played once more, the lights raised and the women could be seen in long skirts and petticoats that were coloured red, white and blue. As the music built, the ladies bent down and took hold of the bases of their petticoats and continued to lift their skirts to the height of their shoulders, displaying their black stockings. Gasps could be heard from the crowd. Then, in unison, the dancers proceeded to kick their legs. After approximately a minute, a line of men, also dressed in red, white and blue, joined in with the dance. The men and women took it in turns at the front of the dancefloor, showcasing their high kicks and cartwheels as part of a choreography that was incredible to watch. In its entirety, the dance lasted nearly ten minutes and saw the line of women and men perform the most energetic routine of the evening. The audience was entranced; even the most disapproving older women could be seen watching in awe as the dancers moved vigorously around the dancefloor. The music seemed to be getting faster and faster, but the dancers never missed a step. As the dramatic finale arrived, the female dancers stood with their backs to the crowd and lifted their skirts onto their backs to reveal their undergarments. The crowd went wild, cheering and clapping erupting throughout the music hall. A standing ovation was given as the dancers gave their final bows; the orchestra too took a bow before leaving the stage. It was now midnight, and with the final performance over, the dancefloor was opened to the public, with many people taking up the opportunity to dance as the orchestra returned to play. Jonathan, Camille, Samuel and Sophia had enjoyed the evening, but decided that now was probably the best time to head home. Sophia quickly went to wish her father a good night, before the four of them left in search of their carriage home.

It was cold outside and Samuel took on the challenge of figuring out which carriage belonged to them, leaving Jonathan, Camille and Sophia waiting by the doorway. The music could still be heard clearly from inside and the cold night air caused them all to shiver as they waited. The music hall had been warm, but the October night air felt bitterly cold. As they stood talking in the doorway, Sophia suddenly grasped hold of Camille's arm.

'Are you okay?' Camille asked, turning to look at the pale Sophia. Sophia held her mouth as though she was going to be sick, before removing her grip on Camille and cradling her pregnant belly. 'Sophia?' Without warning, Sophia's legs buckled from beneath her but Jonathan managed to catch her before she hit the floor.

'Quick, find Samuel,' Camille shouted at Jonathan, and after laying her carefully on the ground, and he ran off into the dark in search of Sophia's husband.

Chapter SEVENTEEN

Samuel didn't turn up to work the next morning, and the tram journey to the warehouse felt like one of the longest journeys Jonathan had taken in his life. His thoughts were fixed on Sophia and the unborn baby.

Samuel had taken Sophia in a separate carriage to Lariboisière hospital last night, which was only minutes up the road from the Moulin Rouge; he had insisted Jonathan and Camille ride home, promising he would let them know any news as soon as he could. Reluctantly they returned home, although neither of them slept much that night through sheer worry. When Jonathan arrived at work that morning he was greeted by Lyle and René who were already there. They immediately questioned where Samuel was. Jonathan relayed the story of what had happened, but whilst doing so noticed that Monsieur Baudin was not in the office as normal.

'Have either of you seen Monsieur Baudin this morning?' Jonathan asked. Both men turned to look through the office window and replied in unison: 'no.'

That morning was the quietest it had ever been in the warehouse; all three men barely spoke as they conducted their work. Jonathan had two trams lined up ready to be serviced, and these almost kept his mind occupied for the entire day. Yet despite their hectic schedules, the three men were clearly worried about Samuel and his wife, and a dark cloud seemed to hang over them all.

Home time could not come quickly enough, and Jonathan almost catapulted out of the door. Walking back along the street towards the entrance to the apartment block, Jonathan spotted Samuel unlocking the building doors up ahead.

'Hey, Samuel!' he shouted, and sped up to catch him. Samuel saw him straight away and waited. 'How is Sophia?' Jonathan asked, finally catching up.

Samuel, who was balancing shopping bags on his arms, did not immediately answer as he concentrated on locking the door behind them. 'Let me help with that.' Jonathan took the key off Samuel and re-locked the door, before dropping the key back into Samuel's hand.

'She got home this afternoon. They checked on the baby and it is fine. Sophia had some checks and they think exhaustion was the cause of her collapsing.' Jonathan took one of the shopping bags from Samuel and they ascended the stairwell. 'My mother and father were looking after Frédéric last night, so he has stayed with them for today and they will bring him home tomorrow. Sophia needs her rest for today.'

'I am so pleased to hear they are both okay,' Jonathan said, helping Samuel into his apartment and handing over the bag. 'Camille and I have been so worried sick since we left you last night; I will have to let her know.' Samuel stopped what he was doing, turned to face Jonathan and smiled. 'What?' Jonathan asked.

'The way you speak about you and Camille is

177

very similar to how I speak about myself and Sophia.' Jonathan smirked. 'Have you told her how you feel?'

'How can I?' he said, deflated. 'It is complex my even being here, and I worry that getting too close to Camille would make it worse.'

'But you are still here, despite only supposedly staying for a couple of nights. How long has it been now – nearly four months?'

'Just over four, yes. But after all this time I would feel foolish to tell her that I loved her.' At that moment Camille walked around the corner, her face a mask of shock.

'What are you doing here?' asked Samuel, shocked to see Camille in his apartment.

'I knocked on the door to see if you were home and Sophia let me in. I have just been helping her into a clean nightgown.' Her gaze fell back upon Jonathan, who avoided her eyes.

'She is comfortably in bed, so I will leave. I am pleased she is okay, but please Samuel, make sure you get some rest too.' Camille smiled at him and squeezed his hand gently as she walked past and let herself out. Jonathan gave his friend a friendly pat on the shoulder and followed Camille.

'Are you not going to say anything about what you heard?' Jonathan said as the door closed and they stood in the stairwell.

'What do you expect me to say in front of Samuel?'

'We are not in front of Samuel now. Surely you must be thinking something?'

'I am thinking you are an idiot!' Her words echoed through the draughty stairwell. 'How dare you tell Samuel that you love me?' Jonathan was speechless. In one large stride he approached Camille and swooped her up into his arms before kissing her on her lips. She allowed him for only a moment, before pushing him off her and slapping him across the face. Without another word she marched for the apartment door, swung it open and disappeared inside, all the while trying to hide the smile that was creeping onto her face. Jonathan let out a small laugh.

Olivier arrived home just as Anne was serving dinner. He seemed in an excitable mood as he dropped a newspaper on the table.

'Is everything alright?' asked Anne, her brow raised.

'There is excitement in the air my love,' he replied, sitting down and pouring the wine.

'Do tell us Papi.' Camille, who sat opposite him, held out her glass to be filled.

'As you know, the world fair ends at the end of this month, and will be officially closed by a cannon shot from Eiffel's tower at six o'clock on the thirty-first.'

'That hardly seems very exciting does it?' Anne sniggered. 'Especially considering we have known about the closing date of the fair since last year.'

'Listen to this; it has been printed in today's paper.' He unfolded the large paper and proceeded to read the following.

This month sees the official closing of The Exposition Universelle, which saw the marking of the 100th anniversary of the storming of the Bastille. The fair will come to a close in honorary style at 6pm on October 31st and will be signalled by a cannon fired from the first deck of the controversial Eiffel tower.

The tower creator Gustave Eiffel will be present at the event, as well as all the fair organisers. Also in attendance will be HRH Edward Prince of Wales and his wife Princess Alexandra, as well as senior members of French parliament.

The 1889 world fair has been the most successful ever held in Paris, and has so far brought thirty million visitors to the city. Now, as the curtain falls on the world fair, we as Parisians will remember this exposition as one of innovation. This has certainly been a monumental year for Paris, and despite the controversy, Monsieur Eiffel has made his tower a city landmark that has proved to be a roaring success.

Olivier dropped the newspaper back onto the table with a satisfied grin upon his face.

'The Prince of Wales is coming again to the Exposition, how exciting.' Anne clapped, 'We will have to go down and see if we can get a glimpse of him.'

'No need my dear,' Olivier said, sounding pleased with himself, 'a few days after the cannon fires there will be an official closing ceremony and the Exposition committee are hosting a dinner which the Prince has agreed to attend. As my wife, you will be proudly at my side.' Olivier had never looked so delighted, and sat in his chair at the end of the dinner table, an almighty grin spread across his face, his enormous moustache twitching.

The entire evening was spent listening to Olivier talk about the exposition. It was the most Jonathan had ever heard him speak. Even Anne struggled to get a word in, which was even rarer.

After dinner, Camille decided to take Jack for a walk. He had been fast asleep under the table the entire evening and was extremely excitable when she picked up his lead.

'Jonathan would you like to join us?' Camille asked whilst clearing away the final dishes.

'Certainly.' Replied Jonathan, and without delay he was on his feet and fetching his coat. The walk was only short, and the dark nights were fast drawing in.

'I am so pleased Sophia is alright.' Camille said, holding onto Jonathan's arm as they walked along the quiet street. 'I am delighted to hear the baby is okay too.'

'It was certainly a fright, it really puts things

into perspective when something like that happens.' Jonathan replied. As they made their way back along the road, rain began to fall. Softly at first, but it quickly turned into a raging downpour. Jonathan and Camille raced the final few feet to the door and unlocked it as quickly as they could. Inside, and with the door locked and secured, they couldn't contain their laughter; they both looked as though they had been swimming in the British channel fully dress. Jonathan raised his hand gently to Camille's faced and brushed aside some stray hair that lay windswept across her face.

'I must look terrible.' Said Camille, 'Especially if the rain has made you look that bad.' She giggled.

'You look beautiful,' Jonathan's expression had never looked so serious, 'but then again, you always do.' Camille blushed, a smile creeped out from the corner of her mouth. As they walked back up to the apartment door, Camille turned to Jonathan and kissed him on his lips. It lasted only a second, and Jonathan's mind filled with the image of the carousel. It had been weeks since he had bought a newspaper, and longer since he had been into the city searching for it. Why would it now come into his mind?

Chapter EIGHTTEEN

Samuel returned to work on Tuesday, and Jonathan was pleased to see him back to his normal positive frame of mind. Sophia had had a good night's rest, and Frédéric was due to be dropped off home by Sophia's mother that very afternoon. Every day that week Jonathan asked after Sophia, and was pleased to hear that by Friday she was back to her old self.

Both Jonathan and Samuel decided not to join Lyle and René at the pub that Friday. Samuel wanted to spend time with his pregnant wife, and Jonathan wanted to take advantage of Anne and Olivier being out for the evening, meaning he and Camille would have some time alone. Upon arriving back at the apartment, Jonathan was pleasantly surprised to find

Camille already back and cooking them both a meal.

'Do you need help with anything?' Jonathan shouted through to the kitchen, all the while being jumped on by Jack.

'Everything is under control,' came Camille's voice from the kitchen, 'there is wine on the table, you can open it and pour us both a glass. I will be through shortly.' Jonathan poured the wine; a pleasant aroma wafted through from the kitchen, reminding him just how hungry he was.

Camille was not long at all, and before Jonathan had finished pouring the wine she appeared carrying a large oval dish. She served up a vegetable and chicken meal with potatoes and, as an extra surprise, had even brought home some pastries for a little treat afterwards. Conversations between the two of them always seemed so effortless, and after both talking about their days, Camille asked if Jonathan had heard how Sophia was doing.

'Maybe over the weekend we should call over. What do you think?'

'I imagine she would appreciate that,' Jonathan replied, 'Samuel tells me she is not getting far at the moment; I think she planned on a walk to the local shops today, but I believe that is as far as she dares go now until the baby is born. Anne was telling me she plans on making some clothing for it.'

'Yes, she was out at the market only yesterday buying fabric. Just neutral colours for now, until the arrival and then I'm sure there will be all sorts of blues or pinks.' Camille laughed as she thought about her grandmother.

'We should get them something too, but what?' Jonathan was quite excited about the idea.

'What about a toy, or a teddy bear? There is a beautiful toy shop near the gallery, we could go in one Saturday and choose something.' Camille began to clear the table as she spoke.

'That sounds a fantastic idea. Samuel and Sophia will be thrilled.'

With dinner over, Camille made a pot of tea for them to have with their sugar-coated pastries. Just as Camille sat again, there was a loud knock on the door.

'I will go, you stay seated,' Jonathan said, leaving the dining room and heading for the apartment door. Standing in the stairwell was Samuel; he did not say a word but simply thrust a newspaper into Jonathan's hand.

'What is this?' he asked, looking at Samuel with an eyebrow raised.

'Bottom left hand side of the page, the smallest article on the page.' The small print was difficult to read in the dim light, and so Jonathan held it closer as he squinted to read the text.

Parisian favourite Madam Mystic has this week returned to Paris where she continues to amaze paying customers. Travelling alongside her beloved carousel, the fortune teller is expected to be in Paris until the end of the week, when she will disappear into the night and continue her never-ending travels around France.

Jonathan looked back at Samuel, his mouth hanging open.

'There is a small detail I need to tell you,' Samuel said.

'And that is?'

'Sophia's mother has been calling every day this week with shopping and newspapers. The newspaper in your hand was from Wednesday, and if the writer is correct then Madam Mystic could leave Paris as early as tonight.' Jonathan dropped the newspaper, his eyes bulging. Samuel stretched out his hand, gesturing Jonathan for a handshake. Confused, Jonathan obliged and held out his own hand.

'I know this is what you have waited for in order to get home. I won't delay you, but I wish you well and hope one day we meet again.' Samuel turned and headed back to his own apartment. Jonathan was frozen to the spot. Camille was in the dining room waiting upon his return, yet the carousel was sitting in the centre of the city, hopefully able to take him home.

Jonathan slowly returned to the dining room, his face pale.

'Is everything okay?' she asked him.

'Camille, I need to speak with you.' Jonathan pulled his chair around so that he was closer to her, and took hold of her hand. 'I have not been completely truthful about why I am in Paris.' Camille's eyes widened.

'I am listening.' She pulled her hand from his grip and sat back in her chair.

'It is difficult for me to explain, because I don't fully understand it myself.' Jonathan gulped aloud; his mouth was dry and his palms sweaty. The conversation he had fully rehearsed in his mind had gone and he stumbled to figure out what he was trying to say.

'Please tell me Jonathan, you are worrying me.'

'When I arrived in Paris, I told you and your grandparents that I would only be staying a few nights whilst I got myself together. The truth is that no amount of money could take me home. This is hard to believe – I barely believe it myself. I am from the future. My parents have not even been born yet and I somehow arrived in 1889 Paris against my will.' He paused and looked up at Camille, whose face was expressionless. 'I have been in search of Madam Mystic and Le Cheval Carrousel Volant ever since I arrived, as the carousel is the last thing I remember from before I arrived in Paris. You see, it is not money, paperwork or anything like that stopping me from returning home – it is that I am unable to return without the help of the carousel.' Jonathan stopped talking and looked at Camille for some kind of understanding. After a long silence, she final spoke, tears in her eyes.

'And why are you telling me this now, after all these months?'

'That was Samuel at the door; he knows I have been searching for the carousel, although he does not know why it is so important. He has just found an article in this week's newspaper which states the carousel is in the city until the end of the week. It could possibly leave as early as tonight.' Camille covered her mouth with her hand, her gaze anywhere but Jonathan. 'Camille, I need you to believe me.'

'How dare you?' Camille finally spoke again. She rose to her feet, pushing back her chair and went to step past Jonathan, but he took hold of her wrist and stopped her. He opened his mouth to speak when Camille's free hand came flying up towards his face and slapped him hard. Jonathan immediately let her go.

'I knew you would do this. I told you not to allow us to get close to you if you were going to disappear.' She turned her head away and covered her face with both hands, trying her hardest to contain the sobbing.

'Camille, please…'

'No!' She pushed him away from her. 'I knew I shouldn't have trusted you. If you are going to leave then just go, but next time think of a better lie than being from the future.' She marched away and made to leave the room, but Jonathan sprinted after her.

'Camille, please let me explain. This is not a lie, I…'

'Stop! You have said all I need to hear. You have done enough damage here already.' Her eyes darted around the room. 'Jack!' she shouted, and the little dog came flying into the room, his tail wagging. 'I am going to take Jack around the block, you better not be here when I return.' Camille stormed out of the room, leaving Jonathan speechless. He listened to her sobs echoing through the apartment, right up to the moment she slammed the apartment door shut.

Chapter NINETEEN

Jonathan stood paralyzed. In his mind, he knew that his longing to return home was what had kept him going, but he couldn't leave things like this with Camille. His eyes began to fill with tears.

He went to his bedroom and changed into something warmer. He then retrieved the money he had saved over the last few months; he had been keeping it in the bedside drawer for safety. It was a considerable amount, and he had been planning to use it to move into his own apartment if he couldn't return home first. He carried the large envelope of money into the dining room, and after finding a pencil, he proceeded to write a small note.

To Anne & Olivier,

Firstly, I must apologies for not seeing you before I left. It was not my intension to leave without saying a proper goodbye. Thank you for taking me in these past five months, I will be forever grateful. As gestures of my gratitude, please accept this money – it is everything I have been able to save whilst working at the warehouse. I will not need it where I am going.

You will all be forever in my heart.

Jonathan.

Jonathan wiped the tears forming in his eyes, sealed the envelope and placed it upon the table. He left the keys and made his way out of the apartment, down the stairs and back out onto the street. He was hoping to see Camille walking back to the apartment – he had to convince her that he was telling her the truth. But she was nowhere to be seen, and the small green across the road was empty. Hesitation in his step he decided to go, and he took off along that road at speed; using his sleeve to wipe away the tears that glazed his vision.

He wasn't sure exactly where the carousel would be located, but decided to go back to the spot it had first dropped him in Paris. It was already getting late, and the dark city streets were beginning to quieten. The tram into the centre of the city barely had a handful of people on board. Despite him now knowing the journey so well, tonight it felt strange to him. With sadness he watched as Paris passed him by, lit up in the night and still so full of life. He knew he could return to Paris any time he liked, but would modern day Paris give him what he really wanted?

When the Eiffel tower finally came into view, Jonathan dismounted the tram. Before starting his search for the carousel, he paused for a moment to take in the giant structure one last time. It was certainly an interesting monument, and although the Paris he stood in did not know it, he smiled at the knowledge that it would still be standing over 120 years later. Jonathan took off along the road and began his search for the mechanical ride, and it didn't take him long to find it. Nestled between the rows of trees, as though it had never once moved since dropping him here almost five months ago, it sat in the darkness, lifeless. It was unmistakably the same one, and even through the darkness Jonathan could make out the gold letters at the top which read 'Le Cheval Carrousel Volant.' Hesitation set in as Jonathan slowly walked closer towards it. The moonlight shining down provided enough light for him to see the beauty of the wooden horses that were motionless on their poles. They looked almost real. Approaching the carousel, Jonathan felt a sudden wave of emotion; he'd never really thought he would see it again. Less than a foot away Jonathan stopped. His mind was racing so fast the city sounds seemed to mute against his own tidal wave of thoughts. The silence was broken by footsteps behind him. 'Camille?' Jonathan said, turning – but it was not Camille. As he squinted through the dim light, Jonathan was shocked to see the old beggar woman he had encountered the night of the art show back in June.

'Good evening young man,' She croaked, her breath visible in the cold air, 'what brings you out at this late hour?' Her smile told Jonathan that she knew exactly what he was up to.

'Are you Madam Mystic?' Jonathan asked, and within seconds the old woman burst into a fit of laughter, a spine-curling cackle that rang through the trees.

'Young man, I remember you. But I am not Madam Mystic; she is over there, behind you.' Jonathan spun around and looked into the trees. At first, he saw nobody, but then his eyes fell upon some kind of tall square item chained to a tree. As he strained to see, the old woman continued to speak.

'Madam Mystic is a mechanical amusement device that leaves you a fortune card if you insert a coin.' Jonathan moved closer to take a better look; indeed, it was a mechanical box with clear panels on three sides, behind which sat a robotic woman with a scarf wrapped around her head. Her hand was pointing forwards towards Jonathan, upon it a large jewelled ring, and her neck was crowded with many beads and trinkets.

'Why don't you have a try?' said the old woman. Jonathan could feel her breath upon his neck.

'No. I don't believe in that kind of thing.' Yet Jonathan could not take his eyes off it.

'What could it hurt?' She leant over and nudged Jonathan on the shoulder, pushing him towards the fortune teller. Taking the final few steps, he searched his pocket for any remaining change he had left. Upon depositing a coin, the machinery inside began to creak and a small tune began to play, the sound of a musical box comb and barrel turning inside. Madam Mystic's arms moved slightly and her mouth began to open and close. No lights shone, and after a thirty-second musical show a small card was deposited out of the front and the machinery slumped back into motionless silence. Jonathan hesitated, looking down at the message. He held it up to the moonlight.

'*Sometimes what you think you want distracts you from what you deserve.*' The old beggar woman leaned over to read the note out loud; she smiled at Jonathan. 'She is good, don't you agree?' Jonathan remained silent and rubbed his eyes.

'Who exactly…' he turned to speak again to the beggar woman, but she had gone. His eyes began to scan the surrounding area, but she was nowhere to be seen. Surely she had only just that second stood right next to him – she couldn't have walked away that fast, could she?

Standing beside the carousel once more, Jonathan placed his hand on the metal railing of the fairground ride. It was cold and rusty. Seeing the carousel after all this time felt like being reunited with an old friend; he took in its beauty and gripped tighter on the handle. As he put one foot onto the edge, something brushed past his ear and landed on one of the wooden horses. It was a dragonfly. Jonathan watched as the dragonfly flew up around the centre pole and back past Jonathan into the darkness. At that moment the carousel lit up, and with a loud groan slowly began to move. This was it. With one foot already on board, Jonathan allowed the carousel to take him with it and allowed his other foot to hang over the edge. His heart was racing fast and, as the carousel approached its first full rotation, he knew a decision had to be made. The carousel began to pick up speed, and as the breeze caught him, he thought he heard another sound – a dog barking. As the carousel reached its second full turn, Jonathan saw Camille and Jack running up the dusty track between the trees, Jack barking at the top of his lungs and Camille calling out his name in a breathless pant as she ran, holding up her dress so as not to trip over it.

Without hesitation, Jonathan leapt from the moving ride and tumbled back onto the ground. His feet slipped and he landed on his back. Winded, he coughed uncontrollably as he sat up and tried to see where Camille and Jack had gone. Still on the ground, Jonathan was bounded on by Jack, his tailing wagging, his tongue all over Jonathan's face. Jonathan could not stop laughing. He wrestled Jack off, and turned to find Camille stood beside him.

'How did you know where I was?' Camille grabbed hold of Jack so that Jonathan could stand.

I found the note you left my grandparents. It was touching, but I was more shocked that you had left all your money behind. It didn't make any sense. So I knocked on Samuel's door and asked him what he knows about the carousel.'

'What did he say?'

'He told me you had been searching for it since the day you arrived; he told me he'd never asked why but had agreed to help you. So I told him what you told me.' Jonathan's face fell. 'He did not know if your story was true, but he told me that he knew how much you loved me and that telling me the truth was probably harder for you than keeping the secret.'

'And is that what made you believe me?'

'It didn't, but something else Samuel said to me made me realise that leaving things how we did was probably not the best idea. So here I am to end things how they should have been ended.' Tears began to fall down her face. Jonathan took hold of her hand. 'Jonathan, I know you told me you loved me, and I didn't say it back because I was afraid, but I need to tell you now before you go that I do love you, I have loved you for quite some time, and if going home is what you want then I will wish you well.' She turned her face away as she tried to hold back her tears.

'Camille you need to know that I never meant to hurt you. I stopped looking for the carousel nearly a month ago as I believed it to be a lost cause. But when I heard it was back in Paris, the thought of seeing my family came flooding back and all I have ever wanted was to see my parents again. But something has changed, and the journey down here this evening has been torture. All I could think about was you, and all I wanted was for the carousel not to be here so the decision would have already been made.' Camille turned back to Jonathan and leaned into his embrace, her tears wetting Jonathan's shirt.

'Why don't you come with me?' Jonathan wasn't really sure why he had said that, but knowing this was goodbye upset him more than anything in the world. Camille backed away from Jonathan's embrace and wiped away her tears.

'Jonathan, you know I don't belong in your time. I belong here, with my grandparents. I wish I could ask you to stay, but that would be selfish on my part. I know if I had the opportunity to see my parents again I would take it, and I do not hold anything against you for wanting to do the same.' Camille gave a squeeze to Jonathan's hand. 'Goodbye,' she said, her voice cracking.

'Goodbye,' Jonathan whispered. She let go of his hand and turned to leave, calling out to Jack who ran ahead of her back towards the road. Jonathan watched her for a moment, his own eyes flooding with tears upon hearing her gentle sobbing. He turned to face the carousel and looked up at the enormity of the structure. It was an attractive piece, and the handrail he took hold of felt ice cold against the palm of his hand.

'I would be stupid to give up everything I have here,' said Jonathan aloud. 'I have a job, and friends and more importantly I have… you.' He turned quickly on the spot and almost ran back towards Camille, who had come to a halt across the grass. He pulled her close and gently raised her face to his own, and he pressed his lips softly onto hers. 'You're cold.' Jonathan drew back and looked into her eyes. 'Let's go home.' He kept his arms tightly around her shoulders. The Eiffel tower loomed above them as they walked along the street, a smile spreading across Jonathan's face, Camille's arms tightly around him.

EPILOGUE

Sophia topped up everyone's wine as the final few minutes approached. Sitting in Samuel and Sophia's sitting room, the four of them watched as the clock approached midnight and the New Year got closer. With less than a minute to go, Samuel stood.

'This has certainly been an interesting year for us all, with Jonathan coming into our lives, and a new arrival due to arrive in January for me and Sophia. I am certainly going to remember 1889 as a good year.'

'Here, Here.' Jonathan hollered.

'Look at the time,' Sophia called, and the four of them turned to see the large clock on the wall counting down the final few minutes of the year.

'Ten, Nine, Eight…' they all counted in unison, 'Seven, Six, Five, Four…' Sophie trailed off and gave out a loud groan.

'What's wrong?' Samuel was by her side in less than a second.

'I think my waters have just broken, our baby is coming,' she managed. Jonathan and Camille raced to her assistance and helped her to her feet. As soon as they got her to the bedroom, Samuel used the communal telephone located at the bottom of the stairwell to call the midwife.

It was nearly two in the morning when the midwife finally arrived, by which time Sophia was already prepared to push. Camille stayed for support, but Jonathan and Samuel waited outside the bedroom in the sitting room. Over an hour later, the midwife finally emerged, and Camille followed behind.

'Congratulations,' the midwife smiled, 'your wife is doing fine and I am pleased to tell you that you have a healthy daughter.'

Acknowledgements

I would firstly like to thank my long suffering husband, who reads my stories so many times. Your support and encouragement is a blessing

I would also like to thank my editor Fred Johnson. Not only did you help polish the story and help make it great, but your encouraging words made me fall in love with the story and characters all over again.

A special thanks goes out to some incredible authors who have become more than just colleagues but friends, mentors and a great support network – DM Singh, Rose English, Maria Gibbs, Joseph Hunt, Claudette Malanson.

Finally I want to briefly mention the November 2015 Paris attacks. I heard about these whilst writing scenes for Carousel, and my heart goes out to all those who lost loves ones on that frightful night.

Thank You!

Time for Paris

Writing Carousel was a pure delight. After finishing The Vintage Coat I swore I would never write another time-travel piece again…and yet here we are.

I have always had a love of Paris, and have had the pleasure of visiting the city twice. I had wanted to write a story set in the city for some time, but nothing stood out to me as to what it could be about. Then I had this strange realization…what would it be like to go back and see the site of the Eiffel tower before it was built. Naturally that would have been a little boring for the book, but after some research I found out the Eiffel tower was built for the 1889 world fair…how did I never know this?

Soon the ideas for a book were coming in thick and fast, but I still needed to find a way to send my main character back in time. I had already used a Coat. Then I remembered my first visit to Paris with my parents, our holiday was mostly based around Disneyland; but on the day trip to Paris I remember standing under the tower with such awe. Across the road was the most beautiful carousel I had ever seen, and naturally my brother and I had a ride. Thanks to this memory I knew that a carousel was just the mode of transport I required.

It wasn't until I was half way through writing this story that I learnt another amazing fact about 1889 Paris. It was also the year that La Moulin Rouge opened. As one of the most iconic buildings in Paris, maybe even the world, I could not pass up the opportunity to have it feature in the story.

1889 was certainly an exciting year for Paris, and if I could personally time-travel then I think it would certainly be at the top of my list.

About The Author

Chris Turnbull was born in Bradford, West Yorkshire, before moving to Leeds with his family. Growing up with a younger brother, Chris was always surrounded by pets, from dogs, cats, rabbits and birds…the list goes on.

In 2012 Chris married with his long term partner, since then Chris has relocated to the outskirts of York where he and his partner bought and renovated their first home together.

Chris now enjoys his full time employment at the University of York and spends his free time writing, walking his Jack Russell, Olly, and travelling as much as possible.

For more information about Chris and any future releases you can now sign up for newsletters by visiting:

www.chris-turnbullauthor.com
facebook.com/christurnbullauthor
Twitter: @ChrisTurnbull20

If you enjoy a book, please take a couple of minutes to leave a review on Amazon. It lets the author know that their hard work wasn't wasted.

The Storm Creature
By Maria Gibbs

At eighteen, Lucy had everything going for her: a supportive family, a rapt audience, and her dream of becoming a published author about to be realised.
A single moment in time on a dark, rainy road changes things forever.

That was then, but this is now. Lucy has suffered through eight years of haunting visions and thoughts with every raging storm thanks to a tempestuous storm creature who torments her. What does the baleful creature want with Lucy?
Will the troubled woman ever be able to let go of the past and forgive herself?

Or will she sacrifice everything she holds dear?

Find out more about Maria and her books by using the following links:

https://gibbsdream.wordpress.com

facebook.com/gibbsdream

twitter.com/gibbsdream

Printed in Great Britain
by Amazon

27339157R00128